JEFF LEE

The Speed of Light

Maybe if we go fast enough,

we can live forever?

1

Landing in Monaco

From here, the whole city can fit into the palm of my hand.

The small speedboat is gliding on the surface, taking us into the arbor.

"Isn't she a beauty?" shouts Marcus over his shoulder while adjusting his sunglasses.

He's talking about Monaco.

The Fortress.

The sea is getting agitated as we prepare our approach, so I clench to the stern.

"And look at these creeps!" he adds, pointing at the rest of our support team already massed on the docks and waiting for our arrival. Media people, photographers and various chaperons sent over by upper management.

"Look at that. Crabs in a bucket." continues Marcus, waving his hand back at them like a four year old.

"They're all here for you Marcus. I'm just riding your coattails," I tell him.

See, Marcus is the champion. The Formula 1 Grand Prix winner of the last two seasons. Plus, he's currently at the top of the standings, and we're already past mid-season.

The skipper slows down as we enter the arbor.

"You hear that Marcus?" I shout from the back of the boat.

Marcus smiles, refreshed.

The violent sounds of the race car engines escape over the walls of the fortress.

"That's the sound of money," I tell him.

Marcus and I are racing partners and form one of the most lucrative racing teams on the planet. A top tier sport franchise held by an alliance of rich investors. An F1 racing team is comprised of two super-fast and exotic horses, which combined with a handful of world-class engineers, might have a shot at delivering massive returns on investment.

As *driver number two*, and also as a good team player, my job is mostly to ensure that my champion's back is covered at all times on the race track. Making room for Marcus to pass a rival and sometimes guarding the passage against a black bishop who's rapidly closing in on the chessboard.

Back in the pits, the Captain sees everything, and whatever the Captain commands from inside my helmet, I must deliver. And I'm totally fine with that.

As long as Marcus is winning, no one is asking me any questions.

And don't get me wrong here. They still pay me millions, plus the same cash amount matched by the sponsors. I still get to enjoy the perks, the traveling entourage, and the accolades. It's just that in my particular case, no one really expects me to save the day.

Best to be next in line than on your way out.

As we glide closer to the dock, the young skipper elegantly maneuvers the speedboat in his final attempt to impress us. Securing our place on the moodboard.

Now before we go any further, I suggest that you take a deep breath.

Because as soon as Marcus and I put a foot on this dock, the bomb will start ticking. We are about to dive into the biggest Formula 1 weekend of the year, The Monaco Grand Prix. And for the next 48 hours, nothing or no one can stop this train.

The Monaco Grand Prix is one of the most romantic, elegant

and yet tortuous events of the season. The circuit features narrow streets, sneaky bottlenecks, technical lower speed sections and several blind curves.

Over the years, enthusiasts, analysts, and worldwide online sports bettors came to learn and appreciate the fact that in Monaco, the action is rarely settled up until the very end.

We both jump off the boat.

The whole dock has been covered with a thick red carpet on which our Gucci loafers slide perfectly. A pair of sharp scissors cutting through the gift wrap.

We are safe here, for now.

Each of the racing teams are given a private dock from which the pilots and the VIPs can shuttle from their hotels to the paddocks by a sea corridor. Therefore circumventing the growing daily flocks of fans and casuals caged back onto the boardwalk. Reaching the holy site without ever touching ground among the infidels.
All super hermetic really.

Now try to picture this.

Whenever we travel from city to city during the championship season, each and every Formula 1 racing team will bring aboard at least a dozen engineers, as many or more mechanics, the pit bosses and the rest of the support team.

From the get go, management will only hire boys and girls coming straight from MIT or the dark web. Most racing teams also bring their own cooks, massage therapists, trainers, PR and content creative kids. Add to that the local fixers and the translators, depending on the country and human rights framework we have to deal with.

A whole village constantly on the move.

Same faces, different Marriott.

Packing and unpacking as we cycle the backdrop.

Meanwhile, the super rich are taking over the air. Over the span of the weekend, the Monaco heliports will receive helicopters at an interval of every 20 minutes. Rich pricks from all over the continent will flock in for 48 hours of party and plunder.

Same faces,
different Marriott.

I've read somewhere that when the race comes to town, the price of tuna tends to fluctuate. Cocaine and sashimis. That's the real med diet.

Don't tell anybody, but this world, it's everything that I hate.

Every weekend, I need to risk my life in order to secure the money. And these rich assholes think they can just *pay to play* with us?

A velvet rope clicks and the red carpet turns to cobble stones.

We have arrived.

"I can smell you Céline, you know?' shouts Marcus. "Talk to me."

We're all walking fast, flanked by a semi-circle formation composed of our management team.

"Let's go over the schedule real quick please, I can't wait to hit the pool at the Villa." continues Marcus.

"We have a pool right? Céline?" repeats Marcus.

Céline shifts gears and catches up: "Yes a pool, indeed, my lord."

"We have a Villa?" I ask both of them, surprised.

"Oh they haven't told you yet?" asks Marcus, amused. "The royal family is hosting us this year. The Prince himself hooked up Céline with the royal property manager or something. Supposed to be all taken care of" he explains.

"Fuck yeah," I tell him.

"They got you a nice perch somewhere up there with the big birds," says Céline. She then pulls a page out of the thick agenda she always carries around. "Okay, here is the schedule just for today boys."

It's Thursday afternoon. Friday, we test drive. Saturday, we qualify, and finally, Sunday, we race. That should be the schedule. But of course, as usual, the PR team had many other plans for us.

"Today we need to be heading straight to City Hall where the mayor has some sort on brass plaque to unveil. Fifteen minutes top, I promise. It's just a photo op with Marcus and the Mayor," details Céline.

"Okay sure. And when do we get the keys to the Villa?" I ask Céline.

"After our second stop."

I like Céline.

She keeps this show on the road and the emails very short.

Céline pulls out another evil one pager from the brazier she's holding. "We need to show up for *happy hour* at some real estate sales gallery. Some rich developer is hosting a select event for VIPs and international buyers coming to town this weekend."

"Screw that," I tell her, discarding the whole idea with a wave.

"No choice, Nolan. They are sponsors. The developer is launching sales of *The Emerald Tower* tonight," explains Céline.

But I counter: "Can't you just send them the usual cutouts? Like we have in grocery stores for the ice cream collab?"

"Nolan, you know the dance. Money talks. We have to go at least for an hour and work the room a little. It comes from upstairs," she explains.

Fucking rich people.

We obviously had to learn to cohabit, but trust me, we are nothing like them. You can always pay for a better view, doesn't mean you get the story.

Marcus grabs me by the neck, twists around and stops to face Céline and the rest of the team. I force a smile to both Marcus and Céline back and forth. "We will all go together," Marcus confirms.

We resume our walk-and-talk, while back there, the entourage is consolidating their powers.

The optics are good right now.

We have arrived at the castle gates, and we were promised safe passage. Paparazzi on scooters and crazy fans are held back to a comfortable distance.

Up the stairs of City Hall, the mayor is already standing on the porch with his hand extended. Flexing a blue three-piece suit that matches my exact same $3000 Gucci loafers. That's interesting. I've never really considered civil service.

And just as planned, a plaque gets unveiled and photos are taken with the champion.

On my left in the media box, I can hear Céline still hammering some details with the Royal envoy, a slim dude with a cool mustache. Probably my age. "Listen, my boys are not super fancy. As long as the ice machine is working around the clock. Also make sure that the cases of Canadian Club we have shipped go through customs and land on the kitchen island. We'll take it from there. And thank you be the way."

She's the best.

"Oh and before I forget, what can we do about the drones?" asks Céline to the Royal envoy. "Do we have a plan to take down the drones from the paparazzi? The boys like to be... *discreet* about their company."

"Yes, yes, yes. Totally understandable. We received your note and passed it down to the royal guards. Now I can assure you *mademoiselle*, that our special forces don't wear funny pajamas or fluffy hats. We hire from the *private sector*," replies the royal envoy, looking at me then at Céline, waiting for some sort of acknowledgment.

"Great," says Céline.

"As you are probably well aware from the tabloids, The Family had its own share of *intrusions* in the past. We simply don't take any chances anymore," tells us the royal envoy.

People who live in glass houses usually have a nice basement.

"So what? You just shoot them down?" I ask bluntly.

"We do Mr. Nolan. We do indeed. And we can do other things, too," he adds, sounding super evil.

I like the Royal envoy. He seems cruel and clean.

"This is a kingdom Mr. Nolan. Never forget," he reminds us.

I slide low-key to my right to whisper behind Céline's ear.

"I like your new boyfriend."

"Shut up Nolan."

2

The Emerald Tower

The Emerald Tower sales gallery is a giant glass box at the foot of the future condo tower, which is still undergoing construction. Reflective blue windows climb up to the middle section while the top floors are still just layers of concrete slabs. A thousand glittering pieces of stone and glass. Some intricate mirror in which I can catch my reflection.

The sales event is packed with rich people smiling and nodding amid platters of seafood being circulated. Some desperate agents are trying to make one more kill amid the busiest weekend of the year.

New faces with great potential.

Céline squeezes into the bar and snaps her fingers at my empty glass. "What are you having there, Nolan?" she asks me, waving the other hand at the barman. For a short moment, her big agenda is simply resting defenseless on the bar. We could destroy that thing now if we wanted to.

"Tequila and tonic," I tell her.

Compared to most elite athletes, F1 drivers rarely get tested for drugs or alcohol—not until 3 hours prior to a race. And to be honest, these tests are mostly random and never taken seriously.

The cars on the other hand, are subject to a long and rigorous checklist. Management wants us to believe that Marcus and I are some kind of fine breed of racehorses when in fact, we're just dandy jockeys. The technology and the engineers are the real assets on planet F1.

Speaking of which.

"What's up with the cars, Céline?" asks Marcus, crawling his way towards us at the bar.

"The cars have just arrived. Engineers are doing their thing as we speak. Test drives are scheduled for tomorrow morning, so just go easy on the booze, boys," warns Céline. "You know that management doesn't like when you drink too much."

"What is *too much*?" I ask her.

"We're not there yet," she replies with a wink.

I've been a good boy for a very long time. But tonight, it's happening. I grab my glass and take off into the crowd with a set of fresh tires. Marcus clips to my wing, dodging more flying fish.

Some guests and VIPs are gathered around a small-scale model of the project erected in the middle of the room. "You know these models actually cost a little fortune to make?" explains some suit to my left.

I just give him a quick look and zero fucks.

"Like tens of thousands of dollars," he continues.

And Marcus was biting. "Oh yeah? Well, then screw the condos! How can I buy that thing? Put it in my living room." He lowers his sunglasses to look at the gentleman. "They built only one, right?"

I just gave him
a quick look and
zero fucks.

On the other side of the model, I detect Céline closing in with a tall man on her arm.

"Nolan, this is Mr. Tomassino. The developer of The Emerald and our host. Mr Tomassino and his younger brother are seasoned builders here in Monaco."

Kill me now.

Marcus comes to my rescue, shakes the developers hand, then motions as if he was kissing the ring. The developers chuckles. He is ravished. The event sponsorship was probably worth it.

To both of us, Mr. T is just another local developer we get to meet on the road. Soon to be left in our rear-view mirror, forgotten as we move on to the next event.

"Anyone want to see the views from up there?" the developer asks.

"We're not really in the market," I reply bluntly. Uninterested.

"People always think they're not in the market. Until they are, Mr. Nolan," lectures Tomassino.

"All right, all right. We could all use some fresh air right now," says Marcus, deciding for both of us. "Let's go up and see if the sky is more blue once you make it to the top."

And we all start moving in the direction of the elevator. Céline, who still has not let go of the developer's arm, leans into my ear, "Try to behave, Nolan. The brothers are heavy around here."

And up we go.

The construction elevator climbing the center shaft of the tower takes us directly to the top floor and opens up on a vast concrete surface with yet no windows nor safety railings. Nothing to stand between us, fragile mortals, and a 45 floors free fall on all sides.

Back when I was a kid, I was super afraid to even hold the rope of a kite. Afraid I would take off in the air at any moment and float away with a sudden gust of wind. Therefore, I didn't venture towards the edge of the tower. I was comfortable right where I was, right in the middle. Right behind Marcus.

"Just don't look down" tells me Céline, well aware of my Kryptonite.

A couple of seagulls laugh in the distance.

"Look at the ocean!" says Mr. Tomassino.

It's called *the Mediterranean Sea,* you dumb wit.

"This entire floor on which we are standing right now is being sold as one unit. It is the crown jewel of The Emerald Tower and delivery is planned for the end of season," explains the developer.

"Asking price?" joins Marcus, playing along.

"Twenty million. That is Euros, indeed," replies Mr. T.

"And what are the finishes? How's it gonna look?" asks Marcus, jerking him around a bit more. Nothing wrong with a little fake business.

"Oh, we deliver *on the slab.* Buyers usually prefer to bring up their own designers and team for the interiors," explains Mr. Tomassino.

"Okay, so top of my head, an extra five million. I see," says Marcus, this time fainting calculation.

For sure Marcus has this type of cash laying around. Ten years my senior and finishing amid the top five every year, Marcus has managed to amass a little fortune for himself. Yet as much as we might enjoy Monaco for a weekend, it doesn't mean we would like to own a piece of it.

It's way more fun if we just go in and out, animal style.
Eat the whole town and let them all fight for the wrapper.

"We haven't seen your brother yet, Mr. Tomassino" asks Céline. "Is he around?"

"Oh Angelo! He's here, somewhere. My baby brother is not really involved with the sales. He has to run all the operations on site. Making sure we don't have any, *surprises* along the way. You know, taking care of business," explains the developer

We finally turn back towards the elevator shaft. "Let's go to refill, shall we? Marcus and I still have a good six hours left to drink before the cutoff," I remind everyone.

As soon as we step back into the glass box, we all get separated when a dozen VIPs rush to Marcus for a quick picture. Meanwhile I manage to slide against the wall, mostly undetected. "See you at the Villa Marcus," I shout.

Looking for a way out, I push through a door and all of a sudden, I'm in a kitchen where some kind of *beating* is going down. Two men wearing double breasted suits are busy holding another man with a yellow sports jacket and some tie-wraps around his wrists.

They all look at me. Especially the one in the middle. Happy to catch a break.

Then another short man with his sleeves rolled up turns to me and attempts to diffuse the whole situation. "Nolan! Come, come. We haven't met yet. I'm Angelo Tomassino" he says with a giant smile.

Taking care of operations, I see.

He grabs me by the shoulder with his hand that has no blood on it yet.

"We're all very excited about this weekend, you know? Lots of action in town, am I right? Lots of action." He then slowly guides me towards the exit. "We're just wrapping up a *little* something here, but we will meet again very soon my friend. Very soon. I promise." Then he sends me off through the back door and into the back alley.

These two brothers are shady. They might not hide any skeletons in their closet, but I bet they poured a hundred in the foundations.

3

Keys to the Villa

The royal envoy and Céline totally had delivered on their promise.

Our villa for the weekend is perched at the top of the *Le Rocher*. Way up there and deposed on the very last strata of developed land. Our own little weather station floating among the clouds.

The Italian classic revival villa has three giant bedrooms and seven baths. It comes fully furnished with a private chef on call until 11 pm, three house maids and one very tall electric fence.

When I look out the window and into the yard, I'm surprised.

"Mr. the Royal envoy, there is a woman swimming in the pool" I ask, amused.

"Oh that's Natalia. She's a friend of The Family. We have her in the guest house for the weekend. I assumed you wouldn't mind sharing the amenities?" the Royal envoy explains.

"Not at all," I reply, eyes still stuck to what as seen from here, looks like a slender 30-something blonde in a cutout black one piece swimsuit.

"Focus," mutters Marcus, as a reminder to everyone and himself.

Meanwhile, I wave towards the women like an idiot when Céline quickly ruins my moment: "Okay listen to me, Nolan. Listen. We will all regroup here before dinner." Then she turns and looks at Marcus. "The champion and I need to head out for radio interviews."

"You do that," I reply, totally detached, still trying to decipher the swimming pool enigma.

"So take a moment to freshen up or do whatever the fuck you want," says Céline.

I always do.

Céline, Marcus, and the royal envoy skate away on the marble floors, leaving me on the ice with a case of a mystery woman on my hand.

"Oh and there is a *beater* parked in the garage!" shouts Céline across the hall.

"What is it?" I shout back.

No answer. A mystery woman and a mystery car.

Now a *beater* is what we like to call the consumer car that that management will provide when we travel on location. Something we can drive around town. You need to understand that for Marcus and I, anything under a Formula 1 car feels depressingly slow. But we'll settle for a Lambo.

Let's check out the car first.
Once you get the car, you might get the girl.

At the flick of a switch, an immaculate and all white garage appears. Rich people have very clean garages. The neon lights are bouncing on the epoxy and at the center of the room, a mysterious car is sleeping under a bed sheet.

More theatrics.

Rich people have
very clean garages.

I pull up the sheet in order to reveal my surprise. This is not a rental. This is a vintage MGB roadster 1973 convertible. Color green like a cobra. Probably part of some royal collection and stored over here. It surely fits the moodboard.

The paint appears unscathed as I run a shy hand along the fuselage.

"I hope you are well rested."

Walking back outside and into the yard, I make my approach towards the pool.

"I really hope you're not a spy," I ask the woman in the pool. She smiles, elbows on the ledge. "I'm Nolan."

"I know. I'm Natalia."

"I know. Wanna go for a car ride?"

"Do you always go fast?"

"Oh I'm sorry. Didn't mean to rush."

"I meant when you are driving. Do you always go fast? The streets of Monaco can be... *dangerous* at times," she says. Now I detect an accent. East Europe, could be Romania.

She's definitely a spy. I push my luck.

"The sun will be setting soon. Would be a shame to waste the moment."

She pulls herself out of the water in one swift move and sits on the ledge.

"I know a place," she simply says.

4

Driving by the Cliffs

The convertible drives smoothly as we shave the edges off the cliff road, overlooking the sea, and the sun and whole universe we just left behind. Her silky scarf twirls and dances along with her blond hair just two steps behind us.

Natalia had put on a blouse and a bermuda to cover her wet black swimsuit. The sun would do the rest.

Turns out Natalia is a local architect and designer working with The Royal Family and hired to refurbish one of the many villas of the estate. And to be honest, I'm satisfied with her short explanation.

After all, this weekend would zoom by very fast.

"Are you going to that Royal Dinner tonight?" I ask Natalia.

"Who isn't?" she replies. "The whole world is in town."

"They won't leave us alone, won't they?" I ask.

"We are alone *now*." she simply says as she twists to me on her seat like a child. "Right now, it's just us and the wind and the turtles and the evil seagulls mocking that ugly sweater."

"It's Versace." I shrug in my defense.

They keep flying over, trying to get a better look.

"Tell me, if you could live at any moment in history. When would you choose?" she asks.

"Interesting. I would say *the turn of the century*. The Paris Expo, electricity, strange new powers. Everything was more magical back then."

"More *magical*?" she says, smiling.

We don't say anything for a while and that's just fine.

"Are you afraid sometimes? When you're out there on the race track?" Natalia asks candidly. "Many crashes are fatal."

"Over the years, I've kinda made my peace with death."

"Did you really?"

"You have to. Even though it's always there. Around the corner."

She runs her fingers through the back of my hair.

"And if I have to die out there, at least it's gonna be in a giant firework."

"Poetic," she says, with a genuine smile.

"And long after I'm gone, people will remember that moment. The flash and the sound. The joy of the fire."

"Bravo!" she shouts, hands in the air like in a roller coaster.

After gliding down the scenic road—winding on the edge of the world—we finally reach sea level.

"Here! Here! To the left!" she screams, semi-laughing as I poorly maneuver to make the curve at the very last second.

"A little heads up, maybe?"

"Hey you made it, didn't you?" She then brushes my hair as you would calm down a pony.

That last turn reveals a secret enclave in which a blue lagoon is nestled filled with pristine waters. I turn off the engine and motion to the cobra to stay quiet and graze here for a while.

The sun now dips its big toe into the horizon.

All I ever wanted is something simple. Could *this* be it?

Natalia throws her white blouse on the backseat, followed by the bermudas. She then grabs my hand and pulls it toward the rocks overlooking the lagoon water some twenty feet below.

"We have to jump now!" she says.

"Aren't there sharks down there?"

"Yeah, but they prefer Italians, come on!"

Sharks prefer Italians.

And we jump together into the pastel paint, holding hands until the very last moment when our feet hit the water. When I swim back up to the surface, the last and delicate rays of the setting sun are contouring against her soft shoulders. Despite full saturation of the moment, I can detect a clever smile as she closes in.
Everything is so smooth on planet Natalia.

We kissed and made love right there and then.

5

The Royal Dinner

It was a small reception, maybe 400 guests.

Céline, Marcus, and I climb up the stairs of the Royal Palace in full tuxedos, as we're about to receive the golden palm. So many flashes my teeth got a tone brighter.

The Royal envoy has just split to join the rest of the Royal flush inside the ballroom.

Security people are bumping into each other.

"Okay boys here's the plan" declares Céline, still at the helm of the agenda. "This is a public function, don't you forget. There are cameras everywhere and idiots attached to them. All waiting for a fuck up."

In this new magical world, everything doesn't cost anything. But anything could cost you *everything*.

"Thank God mommy is here" says Marcus, looking sharp.

"You're welcome" replies Céline. "Now in about 10 minutes, we will need to circle up to the Royal table and pay our respects to our beloved Royal host. You know, kiss the ring and all."

"Oh yeah, and do they have a *big one* like this?" says Marcus, jazzing his fingers in the air along with his bold championship ring.

"They have *all* the rings Marcus," says Céline.

"Check mate," as I wink to Marcus.

"Then we will all sit together for a nice meal. Our table is over there. Oh and as usual, easy on the booze. You guys will need to be strapped up in the cars and ready to test drive the racetrack early in the morning. Engineers just gave us the green light" explains Céline.

Through the crowd, I can see who I believe is Natalia, standing beside a heavy bundle of red curtains. The whole room is melting velvet under the warm embrace of massive chandeliers.

"Yes, yes, yes, Céline. You have my number," I say, as I excuse myself from the brat pack and begin to walk towards the real prize.

Natalia, now confirmed, is wearing a gold, strapless dress.

"Evening, Nolan. I believe you've already met Angelo?" says

Natalia, introducing me to the short man I saw earlier in the gallery kitchen. The one performing the beating.

Fuck.

"The Tomassino brothers owe a lot to the Royal Family," Natalia says.

"Oh hey, no business tonight," says Angelo to diffuse the tension. "You had a good swim, Mr. Nolan?"

"I beg your pardon?" I reply, a little shell shocked.

"Sunset. At the Villa. You had a good swim?" repeats Angelo.

Okay, we're cool. He doesn't know shit about the lagoon and all.

"Terrific. Hum. Nice place," I tell him.

"In this case, I think you will like the boat," continues Angelo.

"The boat?" I inquire.

"Tomorrow night after the test drives, my brother and I are hosting a little party on our modest yacht" explains Angelo. "You and Marcus are invited of course".

Such a flex.

"Sounds good," I reply, identifying all the emergency exits for.

"Now if you don't mind, I'd like to borrow her for a second?"

And without waiting for his answer, I pull Natalia aside and away. We slide to the left and in the direction of a small cocktail bar in the hall. She wears that clever smile again, somehow mocking me just like the seagulls did earlier.

"You should've seen your face," says Natalia, trying to conceal a laugh.

"What the hell was that? You guys are *together*?" I ask.

"Oh, come on Nolan, you're new in town. Lots of moving parts," she says.

"Are you guys together or what?" I repeat.

She looks to both sides and tuck her chin under her shoulder for some sort of reveal.

"Relax. It's just business. And don't you have a big race coming?"

"Feels like it has already begun if you ask me."

She gets that humble look on her face. "Listen Nolan, tomorrow when the cars start flying, all the media and the fans and big money will take over the whole town. All of those twists and turns will swallow everything and everyone into a giant tornado that will eventually take you away to another continent".

She hasn't spoken that much so far. Must be meaning something.

"Meanwhile, the rest of us still live in that postcard you send home."

She picks a gold flake from her dress that's stuck on my lapel and blows it away before she closes in.

Meanwhile, the rest
of us still live in that
postcard you send
home.

"The next design project of the Brothers is opening up for bid. And I must do anything I can to put my hands on it. I hope you catch my drift, Mr. Pilot." This time she sounded cruel and hot like the moment I met her.

My lovely spy.

"Fair enough" I concede.

Céline suddenly appears in my side view mirror. "There you are! Say bye bye Nolan. Dinner is served."

In this case, we're talking about a ten course meal from some five star chef they probably keep in the dungeons below and dust off every year for the occasion. Céline quickly takes me by the arm and scoops me away from Natalia in the direction of our table.

I hope the maneuver sparks a little jealousy in Natalia. I might have sounded a little too emotionally available for a moment.

There is enough silverware in this room to equip the whole Kaiser army. Marcus and the Royal envoy already went over the formalities of meeting The Prince, so all is good and quiet on the western front.

Between soup and salad my phone starts to ring. "Here comes trouble!" I tell Marcus with a giant smile as I spring up to excuse myself.

"Who is it?" asks Marcus.

"Who dares?" asks Céline.

"It's just cousin Billy" I tell them, knowing exactly how they will react.

"This idiot again!" says Marcus. "How come he never dies?"

"You have a big race coming, Nolan. Don't fuck up this time."

Céline is referring to a time in Japan when Billy and I woke up in a different time zone fifteen minutes before qualifications. Call it jet lag.

I just wink at Céline and roll away from the table after carefully topping my champagne glass with a tablecloth. The universal sign for *I'll be back shortly, losers.* The royal envoy watches me take off with a smirk. I guess you can't make an omelette without breaking protocol.

After the seventh ringtone, I've finally reached the quiet of the outside balcony. I pick up, putting an end to my cousin's agony.

"What's up, Billy?"

"I'm in town, Nolan. And why are you whispering?".

"I'm at the royals for dinner, can you imagine? When did you arrive?"

"Just landed, heading to the Four Seasons. You coming?" asks Billy.

"Can't do, cousin, can't do. We have to test drive early in the morning, you know the rules. But I can pick you up at noon tomorrow once we're all set. How's that sound?"

"Sounds good. Hey, by the way, do you have a *number*?"

I hang up.

Here's the thing. My cousin Billy exists in either one of two states: Either he *has* cocaine or he's *looking* for cocaine.

Fortunately, for him, Billy is very rich. A couple of years ago, Billy managed to build and later flip some sort of TCP/IP phone business operating down in Peru, netting himself a sweet $25M that he now squanders around the globe in search of the fountain of youth.

You could say we both like to go fast.

Once in a while, Billy will fly over to meet us and tag along for the ride over a championship weekend. I was just not expecting him in Monaco but whatever.

Cousin Billy is always the promise of fun.

Except for the fact that I personally workout every day and that Billy doesn't do jack shit, him and I kinda look the same. Probably due to the sports bags he carries in his jacket pocket.

And with most of the attention focused on our golden pony Marcus, it's very easy for Billy and I to slide on the surface of things, undetected. Free to roam and hit the party circuit.

Cousin Billy keeps it street level.

Usually as soon as he lands, the question will come: *Do you have a number?* I can picture him right now already pacing his suite at the Four Seasons. Probably circling the compound, hoping to catch a busboy outside smoking a joint. Trying awkward sign language with the pool bar staff.

We once asked a bouncer in Cannes if he could get us the sweet stuff and the big guy came back with a sugar sprinkler that he proceeded to pour all over us, before telling us to *get the fuck out.* We ran away together on *La Croisette* laughing out loud.

Another time Billy locked himself up for four days in some hotel penthouse down in Mexico City where only the drug dealers would be seen coming in and out of the room. He called them back up so many times that the hotel staff thought that Billy *was* the dealer.

All in all, it's best to give Billy what he wants. Keep on smooth sailing. He's a big boy anyways, and we will all sort this out tomorrow over lunch once I'm done with the test drives.

Oh, Billy.

6

The Speed Tests

In the helicopter that is taking us from the villa to the racetrack, Céline holds a mug of coffee that keeps on fogging the bottom of her thick sunglasses. Two accessories to perfectly match her hangover. That four and half minute flight over the city will save us about one hundred autographs.

Marcus, under the silent cover of his headphones, gazes out the window, trying to regain focus, probably listening to Giorgio.

Knights in white satin. This time in a chopper.

"Did you see Natalia last night, after I left?" I ask Céline.

"See who?" she answers.

"Natalia. Golden dress, vaporous blonde." I snap my fingers. "Stay with me Céline."

Down below, an army of Playmobil characters are busy assembling the paddocks. Running wires through stuff, assembling the bleachers, cordoning off the remaining streets to hold back the peasants. Sealing off any possible escape out of this modern-day gauntlet in which we're about to launch ourselves at 100 mp/h just to begin with.

"She was sitting at the Tomassino brothers table, I don't know."

"And?"

"Then she was talking with the short one for a while..."

"That's Angelo, the evil one. Jesus, were they *touching*?"

"Touching? Nolan, listen, I don't know. It was a party. People touch at parties without really doing so. You know."

Oh, Natalia.

My lovely spy. So elusive.

"And why do you care so much?" Céline asks. "You guys hung out like what, two hours together?"

"What can I say? She got my heart racing" I tell her.

"Just try to focus on the speed tests, would you?" says Céline. "By the way, your idiot cousin called me last night."

"He did?"

"Yeah, he was looking for *the number*," she tells me.

"Oh god. And did you give it to him?"

"Well since it is my job to make all of your problems disappear, I *did* give him the number. Yes."

"Good," I say.

"Good," Céline says, resuming her constant scheming behind the foggy shades.

What can I say?

She got my heart racing.

As we land with the chopper, engineers hold on to their hats.

The two red cars are lined up, side by side in the pits, like two very expensive lobsters. Fifteen million dollars each to be exact. A squad of juniors are still pampering the spoilers as we walk into the paddocks. The whole white gloves treatment.

"Gentlemen, we're good to go," announces the chief engineer.

We call him *Captain*. First, because when Marcus and I are on deck, we only take orders from him. And also, because he sports a mechanical leg. A slick prosthetic from the future that he designed, 3D printed and assembled himself. You could say it gets you a foot in the door when it comes to leading a world-class team with the most sophisticated instruments outside of a space agency.

I look at my watch and it's 8 a.m. sharp.

I wonder if Natalia made it back to the guest house last night. Someone zips me up and throws me my helmet before I smoothly slide into the driver's seat. Well, there is only one seat. And for the next two hours, I won't have time to think about her.

Over the course of a single race, a Formula 1 driver can sweat out up to 3 kg of their body weight. Regardless of what you might think, we are super athletes.

No, we're fucking astronauts.

Taking the back-to-back poundings of a hundred space shuttle takeoffs. Just so you know, the G forces alone can kill you if you lack the training.

Even though you might spot some stickers and the logos of energy drinks slapped on the fuselage of our cars, we don't touch that shit. The message is clearly for you. Sitting up there in the bleachers or lounging on the couch and trying to keep your eyes on me. I got eight speeds forward and only one back.

Marcus drives off the pits first, and I follow.

Then we both start to ride and chase each other like two merry dolphins.

For now, the cars are responding well, so we keep pushing.

The narrow streets of Monaco suddenly feel more like a tunnel, especially each time I break the 200 mph wall on the long stretch of the circuit that the French analysts call *Beau Rivage.*

Fans and onlookers start to gather on the bridges and apartment balconies above us. Vibrations tickling their feet as the cars go right under.

We pass through people so fast the faces stay blurry.

Inside the cockpit, there is nothing to cling onto except for that piece of titanium between my legs.

After a couple of minutes, the time will start to slow down as my eyes ultimately adjust to this new reality. Allowing me to decipher and plan my next moves coming up ahead.

The strange feeling of chasing something that is also behind you.

Coming from inside our helmet radio, we can hear the Captain asking: "How is your car, Marcus?"

"She's fine. She's a good girl," replies Marcus, out of breath but holding on as we keep pushing the cars in order to shave more time off of every lap.

"I can see that!" confirms the Captain.

Back in the pits, the Captain stands in front of the control panel made of eight giant screens displaying the analytics and rendering data in real time coming from a set of three-hundred sensors placed on the rockets. A Formula 1 car on average will generate around three terabytes of data per race.

"It's the crispy ocean air," says Marcus. "I think they really like the beach." Marcus is pushing on the throttle, challenging me to take the next curve slightly faster than our previous lap.

Comfort being just an idea right now.

We will continue like this for the rest of the morning with no major hiccups. The sky is blue, the sun is raging and the tires are sticking to the plan.

When we finally roll the horses back into the stables, Céline stands there, looking at me all discouraged like a stack of old tires.

She hands me my phone.

"Your cousin called you seven times."

7

Scoring Drugs with Cousin Billy

Cousin Billy jumps over the door and into the convertible, showing the valet who's king. Then we both screech off the premises.

"How's the Four Seasons treating you?" I ask.

"It could use some upgrades."

"Where did they put you?"

"They got me on the fifth floor. Nice view and all, but I must crawl all the way down to the pool bar to get myself a drink."

"There's no room service?"

"Yeah but that kinda kills the whole purpose, right?" explains Billy.

"My friend, tonight you'll be sleeping with us at the villa. How's that for an upgrade?"

"You got some ginger ale up there?"

"Got what? Is that a new drug you're on now?" I ask.

"Fucking ginger ale cousin. To mix with the CC. Céline told me on the phone that you guys had shipped a bunch of crates in advance."

Billy has done his homework.

"Ah, the essentials!" I reply, raising a finger to the air like some imaginary wand. The other hand steers the green cobra through the jungle. "I'm glad you stayed faithful to the Canadian Club."

"Always."

"We'll just send someone for ginger ale this afternoon," I tell Billy.

"Yeah, why don't we just send someone?" laughs Billy, suddenly remembering how we usually operate when traveling abroad. A whole entourage of the brightest minds dedicated to resolve the most stupid tasks.

"Now how about lunch?"

"Yeah, about that," says Billy. "I took the leisure to add a small stop on the itinerary. My compliments to Céline. He pulls a piece of paper out from his shirt pocket. "Here's the address. We're late actually, but hey."

I glance at the google map scheme he probably printed out minutes ago from inside the Four Seasons business center that nobody ever uses.

"It's a dry cleaner?"

"Yeah I can see that. Clean is good." He repeats. "Clean is good."

Billy is probably so excited right now because he knows the drugs are coming. Most addicts will confirm: this part is almost better than the high itself.

It is *the promise* of the high.

"Don't you think that *maybe* you have a problem?" I ask my cousin.

"Listen Nolan, I only had a drug problem once I ran out of money."

He's got a point.

The green convertible stops at a red light, and I'm browsing all the tables of the cafe to my left on the sunny side of the street.

I only had a drug problem once I ran out of money.

"Fuck that's her. In the window! " I tell my cousin.

"Who?"

"Natalia!"

I'd like to wave at her, but the light turns green. It's a single lane, and the truck behind me starts honking like crazy; and I need to make a snap decision.

We keep going.

I simply couldn't stop for her.

"Jesus cousin, what has got into you?" asks me Billy, now that we have recovered cruising speed. "You kinda lost control there. Don't you drive a fucking car for living?"

"It's a woman I'm seeing," I tell him.

"Okay... and can other people see her *too*?" he asks.

"Very funny, Billy" I reply, plucking the cigarette he just lit from his lips to throw it outside the convertible. "Yes. People can see her *too*. You will meet her later at the villa."

"Whenever she comes back," I mutter.

After more twists and turns on the cobblestones, we finally reach the dry cleaner. There's a parking spot right in front. How ironic. There is also a police car parked on the left, in which the officer reading a newspaper gives me a polite nod as we walk by and enter the shop.

"Relax" says Billy. As usual, totally oblivious to authority.

"I'm not here," I reply.

Inside, it looks like most of the clothes on the rolling racks haven't seen the outside world since the '90s. A poster for Capri is pinned on the wall and has long faded with the sunlight. Most owners of these garments are probably dead by now. So many lost tickets gone with the wind. I swear the whole place feels like a time capsule.

We walk up to the old lady at the counter.

"We're here to pick up some slacks," says Billy to the clerk.

"What the fuck Billy," I whisper.

"That's what they told me to say."

"Un momento por favor," the old lady gestures.

She disappears into the back, and a man with a yellow sports jacket comes out. Wait, I've seen this guy before. I remember. He was the one with the tie-wraps around his wrists when I stumbled upon Angelo in the kitchen at the sales gallery.

"Gentlemen! You must be Billy! And I see that you brought a superstar," says the dealer.

"I'm not here," I answer, while erasing my face with a brush of a hand.

The tie-wraps on his wrists have now been replaced by a gold Rolex and too many rings.

"Just so you know, there is a police car in front," I warn him.

"Yeah, don't worry about it. They are with us," he answers, adding a wink.

"See? Relax, Nolan," piles on Billy. "They're with us!"

The grim-faced man quickly gets down to business. "So what are we looking for today? MDMA? Gummy bears? Wanna see the stars?" he asks.

"Hum, we'd prefer to stick to the organics," says Billy.

"What? You guys called me for weed?" counters the man, now not smiling.

"Cocaine," says Billy.

"Ah the old faithful!" He smiles again. Then the dealer motions us to follow him into the back. "Of course! Come, come, come."

In the corner, the old lady who is now doing Italian crosswords gets up on cue and goes back to the front of the dry cleaner. Giving us the room.

"Thanks, Mama."

The man turns back to us. "She's moving a bit slow, but she's all there" he says, knocking on his head with a finger.

Returning from a large cabinet, the man carries what looks like a kilogram of blow and puts it on the glass table next to a small scale. "So what is it gonna be today gentlemen?"

"I don't know, is it any good?" asks my cousin. Already negotiating.

Without missing a beat, the man pulls up one of those sharp letter opener and stabs right through the plastic wrap. Why do they always have to ruin the package? Anyways. He shovels the blade into the product and presents us with a nice scoop.

Billy proceeds with inspection, and I do the same.

All systems come online.

"Okay we'll take three eight balls," goes Billy with an executive decision. "You'll be open all weekend anyways, right? So yeah, three eight balls for now. Separate tubes."

I turn to my cousin with a patronizing look, knowing all too well this won't be enough. "We have a yacht party tonight," I announce to Billy.

"*Now* is when you choose to tell me?" he says, super pumped and excited about the future. He turns back to the dealer "In this case my friend, double the order."

Billy then grabs the letter opener from my hand and finishes what's left of it.

Fuck lunch, I guess.

8

Pool Afternoon at the Villa

As we pass through the gates and drive up to the villa, I begin to sense some kind of commotion around the house.

Gunshots.

Up on the front balcony, the royal envoy who is wearing only his swim trunks is flanked with two security details. Both are firing up at the sky with their weapons, trying to take down one more paparazzi drone scouting over the premises.

"A thousand dollars to the first man who takes it down!" shouts the envoy pointing at the sky.

He is quickly joined by Céline, also in her bikini top and a bathrobe flapping open.

"Two thousand!" she screams. Wrapping her arm around the envoy's neck while still holding a bottle of champagne.

"Nice place," says Billy.

Meanwhile, rows of tall cedars are covering up the whole scene.

One of the guards finally gets the shot, and the drone (or what is left of it) falls at our feet the moment we exit the beater. Céline, now ground level, rushes out the front door to claim her prize.

"Are you okay?" I ask her amused.

"Yeah baby, it's play time," she replies, then waving her fake nails at my cousin. "Hey Billy, looking good."

"Likewise," he replies with only his chin.

Everybody likes Billy. He might sound like an idiot sometimes, and yet, he has that twinkle in his eye to let you know he's sharp.

"What about the royal envoy?" I ask her, looking up at the balcony.

"Oh, he's cool. Don't worry about it. He's one of us now. Come inside, boys!"

Céline now waltzes around the villa like she owns the place. "I could use a little straightener though," she mentions not so naively in the direction of Billy.

He has that twinkle in his eye to let you know he's sharp.

Out the window and into the yard, a dozen people are enjoying the pool amenities. All good looking indeed. Marcus is also there, lounging on a pool chair. Still with his clothes on and talking to a brunette wearing red vintage sunglasses and absolutely no top.

"Come on, hit me. What do you got?" asks Céline, crashing on the balcony banquette overlooking the yard and the pool and the rest of the world below.

Cousin Billy throws her one of the plastic tubes of blow then opens up another fresh one just for us. We all do supersized bumps.

Céline is immediately back in charge.

Sometimes you just need to move the mouse a little to keep the screensaver away.

"Should we bring Marcus into the loop?" asks Billy, hinting at the window.

"Nah, leave him alone. The guy is practically a saint," she

replies.

Céline is right. Champions don't do drugs.

Marcus once told me that every summer somewhere in July, Marcus spends an afternoon playing the golf course at Pebble Beach with the ghost of his dead father. The guy will buy the whole foursome and then play all the 18 holes alone.

"More *pasta* for us then," says Billy, double dipping.

As I make my way into the yard where the cool kids are, Marcus stands up and wrestles two of the girls trying to shove him into the pool fully clothed.

"Hey, Nolan! Hold this for me, would you?" shouts Marcus while he throws his wallet at me only seconds before they finally take him down. Loafers, khakis, and chains included.

"Good talk," I reply to absolutely no one.

Making my way across the yard and towards the guest house, I can clearly see that all of Natalia's stuff is still inside. Her black one-piece swimsuit lays on a chair. Empty.

Where could she be right now? Why didn't I ask for her number? Is she with that Angelo prick again? I don't even know my own number. Céline probably has it. Céline knows these type of things.

Yesterday it was so simple. She was just *here.*

Back in my room, I change into my swim trunks. I also take Marcus' wallet and place it into the small safe in the corner. We never know, with that many *casuals* around. Anyways, chances are he won't need it for a while. Everywhere we go, everything is free.

Down the staircase, I join Céline and Billy, now super high, watching tennis in the living room. Both are sitting on the edge of their seats. Marcus also enters the room.

"That's a *rerun*, right?" asks Marcus looking at the TV, clothes dripping wet.

"Yeah, you think? I believe Andre Agassi's ponytail kinda gave that away," mocks Billy, not even blinking.

"The glory days before his mad decent," I tell them.

"Poor guy," adds Céline.

"He should have gone out on top," says Marcus as he leaves, walking up to his room to change.

I can't watch TV right now so I jump into the pool and let the salt water clean my bruises. I look up at the clouds from underneath the surface. My world is suddenly upside down. Where could Natalia be right now? Even though the water tastes a bit like yesterday at the lagoon, it all feels so artificial now that I think about it. Rehearsed.

If only I could float here a little longer, maybe I'd have time to figure it out? But Billy pulls me by the leg and out of my reverie.

"She's not here, is she?" asks Billy

"No," I reply bluntly.

Then my cousin backs off, realizing he just burst my bubble.

Alone, I now walk safely in the shadow created by the tall pines guarding the fence. The only thing preventing the exposed giant stones from turning into glass shards underneath my bare feet.

Once I've carefully piled up a respectable amount of blow on my left wrist, the sandwich I'm holding in my right hand now looks totally defunct of any purpose. I therefore begin to shred it to pieces and feed it to the squirrels who rule this particular part of the garden.

Smart little fuckers. You think you make the law around here?

Céline walks up to me, her hand still stitched to (another) champagne bottle.

"Stop feeding them, Nolan, otherwise they'll keep coming back."

"Yeah. Maybe I want them to come back."

9

The Yacht Party

The Tomassino brothers yacht was everything you would expect from two shady developers who made their fortune selling marble chicken cages to other rich idiots.

The listing sheet should read something like this:

Warm essences of brass and teak wood both hold together this marvel of the 7 seas. Perfect for the nouveaux riches looking to widen their horizon. A total of 12 bedrooms spread over 2 main decks including a front pool and a jacuzzi at the back. This yacht has everything you need to impress your broke ass friends.

The ensemble is very tacky, yet well put together.

All of the forty or so guests and as many staff are now stuck together on this raft for the next six hours. The sea is calm and only rare chops of water cut through the moonlight.

And Natalia is here, somewhere.

Hands in my pocket, I'm in the living room standing in front of a strange painting that has captured my attention. It pictures a girl in a blue dress holding a scorpion in her hand.

"The painting is called *The Sting*," says an old man to my right, wearing an impeccable tux. "They want to sell it, what a pity."

The more I look at the girl, the more she seems to be smiling.

The old man continues with the lore.

"A girl is holding a friendly scorpion in the palm of her hand. A creature capable of giving her both joy and pain at the same time. The venom and the antidote," he explains before walking away.

Interesting.

"The venom and the antidote," I repeat.

All of a sudden, I spot Natalia across the room coming my way. As she slowly walks in my direction, I keep on gazing at the painting, pretending I haven't noticed her yet.

Pretending that I'm not totally obsessed.

"Hey, you" she simply says.

"Natalia. I've been looking for you all day, you know? You totally disappeared."

"Disappeared? It's been eighteen hours, Nolan. What is wrong with you?" she asks, amused.

"You're right, sorry. It's just that time itself seems to slow down whenever I approach a black hole." I reply, laying out my defense.

"Ha ha ha!" she feigns, dangling her blond hair from side to side.

She then leans forward and kisses me. Just like that.

Salty lips. An after taste of the lagoon.

Fuck.

This time I feel something.

But shortly enough, we are joined by Marcus. Natalia quickly goes back into rotation in order to work the room.

"Things are looking pretty good for you, brother" tells me Marcus as we both watch Natalia leave our periphery. He takes me by the shoulder and guides me outside where it's quiet and breezy.

"I've been chasing her all day," I reply.

"She looks fierce. I bet she leaves marks."

I tip my glass to that.

We both stare at the ocean for a moment—a mentor and his apprentice fishing for some nugget of wisdom on yet another yacht party.

She looks fierce.
I bet she leaves
marks.

"Listen Nolan, I've been meaning to tell you this for a while now," says Marcus.

"Here we go," I suddenly laugh, grabbing him by the neck.

"This whole *number one* and *number two* routine..." continues Marcus.

"Hey Marcus, we all need to play our part. Forget about it." I reassure him.

"Well, maybe I should've told you more often, but thanks anyways. For having my back out there every weekend," he says candidly.

"Well, the millions kinda help, you know," I reply.

"You are a great pilot, Nolan. Onc of the finest out there. And you will have your moment at the front eventually. I know because I've been there before."

I reach for the plastic tube inside my tuxedo pocket and allow myself a generous bump, most of it gone with the wind. When I motion with the key to Marcus, he politely declines, apparently not finished with his *exposé*.

He brushes a little white dust from the lapel of my tuxedo.

"Tell me Nolan. Underneath all that crap, is there someone that still wants to win?"

I always liked Marcus. He drives right to the point.

"Of course."

"Then let's fucking show them."

And now with this little locker room speech, I'm feeling super pumped for the qualifications tomorrow.

As we are both here sharing tales of a life of privilege beyond international waters, thousands of people way much richer than us are currently checking in. Filling all the remaining hotel rooms of the fortress up to capacity. Up to the point where the whole thing could burst at any moment.

"Hey, wanna trade watches?" asks my partner.

"Trade what?"

"Trade watches. For good luck tomorrow" explains Marcus. "Saw this in a movie."

"Marcus you're wearing an OMEGA Seamaster Diver 300m Titanium Limited Edition" I tell him pointing at the piece and waiting for him to resurface to reality.

"And?" asks Marcus.

"And mine is a rubber G-Shock I bought on the streets of Jakarta because I liked how the big timer button feels when I practice my breath underwater".

"Brother, you know I always respected the G-Shock. And you know what? I bet there is only one rubber G-Shock on this boat right now."

Champion's got a point.

"Many *Seamasters* maybe, but only one rubber G-Shock." says Marcus.

"All right, all right. Let's switch. But no refunds," I warn him.

"No refunds."

We proceed with the exchange, hug it out, and walk back together into the party.

Tomorrow, I have a strong feeling that we will crush it for qualifications. And now I'm the one looking at my watch constantly, counting on my fingers the hours remaining until the moment I should officially stop doing blow.

We all have our timelines.

With still plenty of room left on the runway, I scrape together what is left inside my plastic tube and begin to look for my cousin, hiding somewhere amid the casuals.

Céline finds me first.

"He's a total idiot, you know that, right?" Céline asks me, tilting her head at cousin Billy, currently super busy polishing some brass rail guard with the sleeve of his shirt. Trying to mirror his potato head in the golden reflection.

"He's just a kid," I shrug. "Let him play with the box if he wants to." Maybe if we were all just a little bit more like cousin Billy, the world would be a funhouse.

Now satisfied with his little experiment and his hundredth selfie, Billy joins us.

The board of directors is now assembled.

"Okay quick tally guys. What's left in the inventory?" Billy asks both of us, skipping formalities.

"I'm all empty," I reply. "Been racing to the finish line."

"Céline?"

"I'm all out too. The royal envoy is really forcing my hand," she replies.

"Does his nose bleed blue?" ask Billy.

"Nope. Mere mortal. Just like us," says Céline, rather disappointed and blowing her cigarette smoke up to the ceiling as if throwing a veil over our next intentions.

"I got two full tubes left. One is consigned at the coat check" says Billy.

I can't slow down now.

"Gimme the coat check ticket," I ask, immediately launching into a side quest.

"You are flirting with the cutoff again Nolan," says Céline, looking up to the heavens and exhaling another big drag of smoke.

Suddenly, someone is dinging repetitively on a flute of champagne. The music fades and the guests start to assemble in the living room. Oh god. There will be a toast. Please just don't mention my name. I'm not here.

"Friends, it's always a pleasure to have you all on board," says big brother Tomassino.

Skip to the part.

"...and my brother and I would like to use the occasion to announce that tomorrow, all the wonderful art you can admire on this yacht tonight, will be put up for auction," he continues.

"Is there anything not for sale on this boat?" I whisper to an NPC standing next to me.

"We can discuss details in private, but for now friends, just enjoy the evening!" says Tomassino, raising his glass.

Natalia, having completed another rotation, grabs me by the arm and with a huge smile on her face, pulls me aside and towards the cabin hallway.

"Come."

She seems familiar with the yacht layout, but I don't wanna know.

Pushing me inside a guest room, she turns the lock behind us and resumes kissing me. The action trickles down onto the bed and we both start to paddle in the same direction. The moon and the stars are the only ones watching through the cabin's porthole.

All I was looking for, is just a room with no questions.
A friendly duel with no weapons.

But as we roll together on the bed, all of the lights in the cabin start flickering.

And then, the power on the yacht totally shuts down.

It's now dark everywhere we look.

We suddenly hear something coming from starboard. A big splash in the water.

I look out the window but there's nothing to see.

"Probably some drunk idiots throwing furniture overboard," says Natalia, trying to kiss me again.

"Furniture?" I ask.

We put a halt to our session and walk out of the room together to investigate.

Outside on the party deck, the music has stopped, and we begin to hear some sort of chatter among the guests that are now massed along the railings, looking down at the water.

"They think someone fell off," says a man to my right.

"Someone?" I ask.

The staff and security are all pointing flashlights at the dark waters around the yacht. The sea is rather calm tonight, and except for the guests whispering among themselves, we can't hear anything else coming from below.

Still holding Natalia's hand and moving back inside, we re-group with Céline, Billy, and the Royal envoy already gathered at the center of the living room.

"Wait, where is Marcus?"

10

The Disappearance

A heavy knock on the door wakes me up.

I hear the voice of Céline.

"Nolan?" she asks.

"I'm not here," I shout from the bed.

"Nolan, two officers are here for you," she says.

Oh god.

Last night, Marcus never made it out of the boat.
And in about five minutes, these two local officers will demand
that I open the small safe in the back of my room.

Inside, they will find Marcus's wallet and also his watch.

Fuck.

As I get out of bed and walk towards the door, I quickly look out the window and across the yard at the guest house. There seems to be no more stuff from Natalia hanging outside. The door is wide open, and the maid is cleaning up the room.

She's gone *too*.

11

Locked up

The cage they locked me into is not super fancy.

It's a dank and rusty dungeon somewhere deep underneath the royal palace. Spooky place, believe me. Even the best set designer couldn't render it that well. Imagine *The Man in the Iron Mask*. Except this time, they lock me into a Suzuki helmet..

If this is going to be my last meal, I'll take a full loaf of white bread with a bunch of garlic butter and a Coca-Cola Classic on ice. Thank you.

No seriously, what the *fuck* is going on?

They locked me in here with no cellphone and no Céline.

Do they really think that I'm the one who threw Marcus overboard?

I was with Natalia, did they at least speak with her?

So... who did it? And shouldn't they be looking for a body right now?

Seems like I totally lost track of time, since there's no window nor G-Shock around. I must have been locked up down here for an hour, maybe more since the moment the two officers scooped me up at the villa. Since they asked me to open that safe.

And what about the qualifications this afternoon? Jesus.

Will they even let me race?

12

10 Years Ago, Somewhere in Suburbia

Back then, we always had a plan.

There was a dollar vacuum at the gas station we spotted earlier that week. Pretty soon, that vacuum would become our first triumph. We quickly discovered that a carefully placed hit of the hammer wrapped inside a t-shirt would break the lock easy on the first try. With just the muted sound of a hockey puck hitting the frame.

That was the first sound of money.

An informant on the inside (my cousin) told us the manager emptied the machine every Tuesday morning. So late at night on Monday when we knew the loot was juicy and all the lights were off, we would make our move.

Of course, I was not the one with the hammer. As the getaway driver, my role was to keep my eyes on the road and on the sandwiches the boys would leave on the dashboard until their return.

Some kind of a reward system and for good luck, I guess.

We would break the lock and steal the money while making sure to leave half of the coins inside of the box. Never too greedy. We would then put a brand new lock on the box, clean everything up and finally place the new key on top of the vacuum. Keep a double of that key for ourselves.

New administration, suckers.

It was genius.

Every week after that, and this time with the proper key, we would come back and collect a little slice of the revenues, skimming off the top. Again, never too greedy. Just a little taste.

New administration, suckers.

Needless to say, once we were satisfied with this pilot project, we decided to scale up the operation over the whole town. We're talking about a dozen vacuums in total here that ended up under our control.

One particular machine near our high school football field was somehow more *generous* in its offerings, week after week. And we couldn't quite figure out why. One day, I decided to drive by during business hours to see what's up. That's when I got it: the vacuum was overlooking the cheerleaders practice field. As simple as that. You bet that some guys would go deep in their pockets to find that extra dollar to keep the fun going.

You wouldn't believe the number of creeps rolling around in a clean car.

Now on a good Monday night, the four of us idiots in a blue Dodge Colt could rack up to $900 after expenses. Mostly for new locks and sandwiches. That was enough *fuck you money* at the time to keep us safe and away from stupid jobs.

You don't really want to be rich. Just richer than your friends.

We were princes of suburbia.

When asked to describe my teenage years in a recent *Sports Illustrated* interview I simply replied: "There's not much you need to know except that I was the guy with the pool."

That's right. Every two weekends or so, my parents would fuck off to play golf or something out of town. That was the signal for my friends and I to get the hot lines going and invite half of my high school to another epic house party. Leaving the other half waiting by the phone for an invite. Probably dreading the stories of battles and conquests these poor fucks would have to endure on Monday morning.

By the way, my parents can never know what we did to that house.

There were so many girls at my parties that my neighbors thought we were hosting a cheerleaders' convention. Never got any complaints. Except for the golf balls they would bring back when the dust had settled. And if a patrol car ever showed up due to the noise, we would offer the cops a couple of Red Bulls to buy ourselves an extra hour.

You see, the boys / girls ratio is very important when you throw a party. A responsibility that I took very seriously, indeed. Too many boys and things start to slip. Too many girls and they all look at each other, thinking it's a trap. You gotta strike the right balance. That way, you keep all the boys in check, and their hopes up.

There were kids in the yard, kids on the rooftop, and cars parked all the way up the curb.

And it is over one of these parties that we struck our next brilliant idea.

We would invite some junior college jocks from the next town over. Then after a couple of beers and shots, they would sooner or later jump into the pool where all the girls were.

Splish splash. That was the second sound of money.

The moment we had the victim exactly where we wanted, one of my associates would identify their pile of clothes, pick up the car keys left inside, and drive away with their car into the crispy night.

By the time these guys would wake up hungover the next morning on my living room floor, the keys would have returned to their pockets, but the car would have been long gone.

Probably half-way taken apart into pieces before these idiots could even say *brunch*.

But this little scheme was pretty short-lived because as you might imagine, we could only pull it off maybe once or twice over the summer. The thing was simply not scalable.

It took us a while to figure out, but soon we came up with a smarter variation.

See, the core idea that makes a good scheme is to know and control where all the pieces are at any given time. In our particular case this meant *the owner* of the car, *the car itself,* and *the people* who were eventually gonna be looking for it.

Again, we had an informant working for the local towing company (my cousin, not the same). And every week, he would provide us with a fresh list of all the cars about to be repossessed. Cars that the towing company would have to seize up and bring back to the lot.

Repossessed meant that the owners couldn't make their monthly payments anymore.

Call it gone in 60 installments.

Therefore, we did not have to *steal* those cars. The towing company would just do it for us and bring them home safely.

The cars would usually remain in purgatory on that secured lot between 30 and 60 days before they either go to the bank, or back to the original owners if they could come up with the money in time.

So here was our plan.

We would take these particular models detailed on that list and start to advertise the spare parts for sale on some dark corner of the internet. And boy, our prices would be *very* competitive.

As soon as someone would take the bait and place an order for a specific part, we would simply go to the lot, pick up the keys from my cousin and take a little ride to the garage next door.

On the table of operations, we would extract the premium part we needed and replace it with some lower tier equivalent that would keep the car running without any suspicions.

Now don't bother me with serial numbers and shit. Technically, we were holding the titles at the moment of the sale. It could take years before anyone would figure something had been swapped inside.

In the end, whenever the bank or the rightful owners would come back to the lot to claim a car, my cousin would give them the keys. They would simply drive off and away with no problems. Never even suspicious that some of the internal organs had been tinkered with and sold on the black market.

We were stealing *from the inside.*

Pretty soon after that, I started to borrow some of these cars for myself.

They were not going anywhere, right? Stuck in limbo for 30 days. I simply did them a favor by stretching their legs a little.

My favorite cars to show up on that list were the BMW M5 2003, the Acura NSX 1991 and the Porsche 911 SC class of 79.

We would drive around town, pick up some girls, you know.

And in my spare time, I would bring some of these exotics down to the local racetrack behind the industrial zone. A beat down rink that had seen more glorious days back when America and power were still about gasoline.

There, I would spend hours speeding around the rink, pushing the cars to their limit.

All I ever wanted was to go fast. Not to run away, just to escape. Get ahead in life. Leave the rest of the world behind. They could try to catch up.

On the circuit, I would usually clear my mind for a couple of laps at full speed then I would stop by the clubhouse to refill with a

$5 giant hot-dog while staring at the memorabilia hanging up to the walls. Sun washed pictures of former local champions, brass trophies next to local paper cutouts. Somehow always laminated too close to the edges.

One of those crispy mornings, I was busy beating the shit out of the silver NSX on the racetrack. The summer was turning into fall and a trail of autumn leaves would fly off in my wake. The cold air was rushing through the engine, providing top performance on the rink.

As I was lapping around, I saw an unusual number of folks and kids gathered around something in the pits.

A lot of action for a Tuesday morning at *nowhere* rink.

When I steered aside to check out what was going on, I suddenly recognized one of the race cars from the pictures I saw earlier in the clubhouse. And the man standing next to the NASCAR beast was maybe ten years older than me.

Apparently, that day he was scheduled to stop by and showcase his car to a bunch of 10th graders on a field trip. The same car he had won the national championship with a couple of weeks ago.

His name was Marcus.

And he looked straight at me.

"Hey NSX guy, wanna go faster?" he asked.

"Fuck *yeah*," I told him.

All the kids were chuckling indeed except for the educator. Marcus then threw me the keys and opened up the door, revealing the intricate inside of the machine. I sat inside, took a deep breath and turned on the ignition.

It was at this *exact* moment that I came online.
That roaring sound. Suddenly, all systems were go.

And these kids knew it because they all jumped out of my way seconds before I pushed the pedal to the floor. Sending black fumes all over the place as I launched real fast onto the racetrack.

First, I took what felt like a victory lap. In the eyes of these kids, I was already a champion.

And then with every loop faster than the previous one, my confidence started to build.

Everything so silent. So clear.

For the first time in my life, I felt I was no longer driving in circles.

"That was pretty good, brother," said Marcus on the way back. "If you ever find yourself in Texas, come see me. I run the new pilots training program down there. We have plenty of toys to play with too."

I had the tiger by the tail.

The next day, I brought the NSX back to my cousin at the lot, cashed out for whatever parts we had left in storage, and finally went home to pack my bags.

I was about to leapfrog this whole fucking town.

Never to be seen again.

Until ten years later, when everybody in town stopped whatever they were doing to watch TV, as I was making my debut into Formula 1. And they kept watching every Sunday after that.

Glad that *one* of them finally made it out.

Alive.

13

Catch and Release

I've read somewhere that in prison, the smell of piss and chicken soup get so often entangled that after a while, both make you hungry.

I've read somewhere that in prison, if you don't get your ass kicked during the first week, it's because the inmates are running an auction between themselves. Trying to establish who will get to ride first on the shower train. Trading cigarettes and noodle cups for your sorry ass.

But as far as I know, I'm the only one locked up down here.

Unless this table can talk.

I already gave up banging on the door after fifteen minutes.

No one is picking up at customer service.

In times like these, I can't help but think about the boys back home that I grew up with. The ones who settled down a little too fast, and now lived comfortable yet uneventful lives.

They had it in their minds, just not enough in their hearts.

Locked up in here, I start to question whether my thirst for adventure might have gotten me a little bit too far? A rare moment of weakness I can't escape.

> They had it in their
> minds, just not
> enough in their
> hearts.

But then, let's face it. If I stayed back home, I would have spent all my Sunday afternoons watching someone else crushing it on TV, while I drank all weekend lying on the couch.

I promised myself I would never become one of them. Just another idiot caught on a loop somewhere in suburbia. Unable to break through the chains of a COSTCO membership card.

That dreadful thought alone suffices to bring me back on track.

Now can someone tell me what the fuck is going on *here*?

Nobody said anything about a lawyer nor a phone call. I thought the Geneva convention would allow for at least a Sudoku or something? I hope Céline got this on the other side.

I hope she's busy beating up these two crooked officers with her thick agenda. Most of it now rendered totally useless anyways, since Marcus has gone missing, and the rest of the assets are frozen in *here*. A sad non-fungible token stuck on the blockchain, yet unable to execute the contract it was programmed for.

Footsteps.

One officer finally comes by and unlocks the door.

He steps inside the cell and glances at me without saying a word. This motherfucker looks tough. Chiseled face, sailor hands. The type of guy that could light a cigarette in a snowstorm.

He stares at me for a second and then steps right back out. Finally, the Royal enters the cell and sits at the table in front of me. "Mr Nolan, I hope this unfortunate episode wasn't too... *uncomfortable?*" he inquires.

"No comments."

"Let's get to the essential, shall we? The clock is ticking," says the Envoy.

"How about a snack first?"

"To speak quite frankly, this whole *disappearance* act is quite *embarrassing* for the Royal Family," he continues.

"I bet it is. Do you believe Marcus is dead? Or has he *resurfaced*? Is there a body or something?"

The Envoy remains unmoved.

"We have no clue at the moment. And I'm also afraid it's just a matter of minutes before someone leaks the information to the press," the Envoy confesses, looking rather concerned.

"What time is it?" I ask.

"It's 9:15. A press conference is scheduled for 10 o'clock sharp. We expect movements, but we hope we can jump ahead of this," he explains. "Céline is working on a statement at the moment."

"Fine. So listen. I don't care about any of that stuff, really. What about the race?" I ask. "Will they even let me qualify this afternoon?"

I have a feeling the Envoy is more preoccupied about the optics than *actually* getting me out of here.

You could say this weekend took a turn, for lack of a better word. Personally, I did not intend to make any waves. I just wanted to be alone amid the usual thousand people. Smartphones in the basket. Dealers on the premises. Now all of this?

"Will they at least let me go through qualifications?" I now plead with the Envoy for a second time.

"Well..." he starts, but I cut him off right away.

"Wait, hold on a minute. Do they really think that I'm *the one* behind all of this?" I ask him, backing away from the table. "For Christ's sake, Marcus was my partner and my best friend. We did everything together. Do you really think I would throw him overboard for some stupid watch and a wallet? Hey, I'm fucking rich too, remember?"

"Please calm down, Mr. Nolan. You are right. What matters at the moment is the race," he finally acknowledges.

"Thank you."

"With all these people in town for the weekend, The Royal Family insists that the show must go on."

"So what's the plan?" I ask.

"You will be allowed to participate in the race. At least for now. At least until the royal guards can figure out what happened to your partner last night. Now before we leave, there is just one thing."

"You want to check inside my lunchbox?"

"They want you to wear this at all times."

And at that moment, the Envoy places a pager-looking device on the table right in front of me. "It's an ankle bracelet," he adds.

"Yeah, I know what it is. I watch CSI too, you know?"

"These are my instructions, Mr. Nolan. And it's non-negotiable," he concludes.

Fucking lizard-man. Cold as ice.

"Until we can figure what happened to your partner, you are not allowed to leave the kingdom."

"Fair enough" I shrug, grabbing the device to strap it on my foot.

Yesterday when we arrived in Monaco, I was a shooting star. Now I guess I'm just a blip on the map.

We exit the royal palace by the big door. The sunlight is brutal, yet appreciated.

Cousin Billy is sitting behind the wheel of the beater while Céline is leaning on the side door, her arms crossed over the agenda.

"Nice Denver booth, Nolan. Does it count steps as well?" she mocks, looking at the chunky apparatus on my ankle.

"Fuck off, Céline. It's a gift from your boyfriend."

"Did you sleep at all?" asks Billy.

"Like a baby. Thanks for the *Xanax* by the way," I tell him.

"No problem cousin. I'll just bill your insurance."

"Any updates on Marcus?" I ask Céline.

"Nothing. The keyword for now is *missing.* Oh god, the press will have a field day with that, I can guarantee you," she tells us. "But the less they know, the better it is."

"Need me for anything?" I ask her.

"Nah, it's best if you just stay under the radar until the qualifications," she replies.

Céline opens up the passenger door of the beater and motions for me to sit. "You guys go grab a bite, and we'll regroup in the paddocks at noon."

"I know a place," says cousin Billy.

14

Breakfast at the Casino

As soon as we step into the casino, they shuffle all the decks. Contrary to us, they don't take any chances.

Billy flips a $20 chip to the first doorman who says hello. Another Scorsese reference.

"You already have chips on you?" I ask my cousin, puzzled.

"Yeah, I came here last night after you guys all went to bed. I was wired as fuck. Couldn't sleep," he says.

"And you didn't cash them out?"

"Why bother? I knew we would be back," explains Billy, as he leans towards the *all you can eat* hostess for a smooch on the cheek, followed by another $20 donation.

"Give us a quiet booth please, lots of snipers around this morning."

"It's not a strip club, you know?" I whisper into my cousin's ear.

"Same economics," he shrugs.

"So tell me, no sleep at all for cousin Billy?"

"I might have blinked for a minute on a pool chair. That's it."

That's it. Classic Billy. Fucking degenerate.

And now that he's been in town for no more than 24 hours, he already dropped at least ten large ones in the joint. The man is quite gracious to watch actually. I like how he uses petty cash to smooth over any logistics.

We follow the hostess down to a section where we can keep an eye on the TV screens. The press conference is about to start, and I believe we're safe in here because nobody has recognized me yet.

I guess morning gamblers only have eyes for the cherry rolls.

"Thank you honey," says Billy, throwing the hostess another cookie.

I like the casino early in the morning because it's only professionals on the floor.

None of that *dinner and a show* crowd that only comes in on Saturday nights with a petty $200 that they slowly pinch inside of their purses in a lame attempt to kill time.

Right now, the overnight cleaning crew is leaving the building. The stalls are sanitized, and the paper towel rolls are crispy. Oxygen tubes have been cycled. Chlorine pellets dropped in the fountains. And all is right with the world.

Doesn't matter if you are black, white, or yellow. To the casino people, we're all green.

Some morning you might spot a salary man getting a close shave inside of the men's room, right before punching into some real job outside in the real world. Pulling out another double shift, yet taking it like a man. It's all for the family.

And Disney World isn't cheap, kids.

Back in our hometown, every casino dealer knew cousin Billy, because he was the jackass doing his cardio around the premises. Jogging laps in the parking lot between blackjack sets. Getting pumped for another three hour session at the table.

Now he's mostly crushing Adderall for the same results, thanks to recent scientific advancements in pharmaceuticals.

We both perform a scouting lap around the buffet before we settle down in the boot. Me with bacon and eggs, and Billy with a full plate of chicken wings. It's a no-fly zone.

My cousin sits down
with a plate full of
chicken wings.

It's a no-fly zone.

By that time, all the flat screens over the bar are featuring a different angle of Céline speaking to the press and flanked by the Royal envoy. Sound is off, but the caption running underneath reads: *Champion is hospitalized due to illness. Doctor still assessing his condition. Marcus might have to forfeit the race.*

Hum, the sick man card. Well played, Céline. That might buy us some extra time.

"What do you think actually happened out there?" asks Billy, stealing one of my bacon strips first. Indeed.

"Man, I don't know. Marcus was talking with me on the top deck for a while. He seemed so happy. We were about to conquer the world and shit. Then I went inside to shag Natalia and the rest of the night unfolded super fast."

"You heard that *splash*?" my cousin asks.

"Yeah, I mean like everyone else on that side of the boat. But as soon as the lights came back up, it was confusion for everyone,"

I recount.

"I've heard the royal guards spent the night combing the whole ship. Didn't find anything," says Billy. "We were kinda far offshore, no? If Marcus fell in the water, the body might take days, maybe weeks to wash up."

On the flat screens, it's now the lizard man speaking to the press. The rolling captions says: The *race will go on. Qualifications start at noon.*

"You think it has something to do with the Tomassino Brothers?" asks Billy. "I mean, it's their fucking yacht after all."

"Well, they obviously have something to do with it. Now it's tricky, because they are tight with the Royal Family and all. The laws of gravity don't seem to work the same way around here. Especially around them."

We go for another lap around the buffet. But the tires screech.

"Oh fuck," I suddenly warn Billy, pointing at someone beyond the bar.

"What?"

"I don't want to see her," I tell him.

"See *who?*" asks Billy.

"Over there. That's Casino Jackie."

Smoothly, I motion to Billy to quickly ditch the plates on the buffet, before walking away deeper into the casino. Hoping we can find refuge in the cheap slots section.

I had forgotten about Casino Jackie.

15

Cat and Mouse

Casino Jackie is a local bookie.

Technically, she doesn't work for the casino itself, but somehow turned the whole place into her base of operations. Not a wager is placed in this town without her knowing about it.

She's tall, slender, and manages to slip into every crack. Picture a praying mantis with cowboy boots. Always lurking over your shoulder when you least expect it.

"What's wrong with Casino Jackie?" asks Billy as we both slide onto a blackjack table.

"She's a jackal; she's a snake."

"She looked kinda hot to me, though."

"Yeah but steer clear. Trust me, she's the devil. She and I had *a thing* last year."

"A *thing*?"

"We hooked up. But she was mostly trying to gain information from between the sheets."

"Cousin, I'm kinda turned on right now," says Billy.

"We have no time to deal with this shit," I counter spell. "We have enough on our plate for now."

"We had," smirks Billy, probably thinking of the premium chicken wings he had to forfeit by the buffet.

See, Jackie is like a human computer. Always calculating and recalculating the odds and whatnot, based on the information she gathers in real time on the casino floor. With all the bets and rumors going through her, Casino Jackie is a dark bridge to the underworld.

We can trust her with the numbers, but for anything else, fuck off.

Some old Botox lady sits next to Billy at the blackjack table. Her whole face is barely held together like a fake sandwich in a fast food commercial. She puts down her phone on the ledge of the table, revealing the picture of a pesky looking dog set up as the background image.

"Nice looking pooch," says Billy, pointing at the *thing* and seeking engagement.

"That's my Moo-moo," replies the old lady, cracking a cigarette voice. "We had to put it down last month, poor thing," she explains, looking rather sad.

"What happened? Cancer?" inquires my cousin.

"New condo rules."

It's 10:25 a.m. and the old lady is holding on to an empty Margarita glass that she waves in the air, hoping to catch the attention of the floor girls. I don't know why we should expect anything different coming from that old sack. She sure knows how to vacation.

"Nolan! She's coming. To your left," warns Billy.

"Oh god. Here we go," I sigh, now with no chance of an escape.

Casino Jackie joins us and slides on the empty stool next to me.

"Oh-hi boys! Too busy to say hello to an old friend?" she says to me.

"Hi Jackie," we both replied together like schoolboys.

"And who is your lovely sidekick?" Jackie asks, taking a curious interest in my cousin. Probably a variable she didn't account for yet. "He wasn't with you last year, am I right?"

"That's my cousin Billy. And no, he was not."

"Permission to touch?" Jackie asks, extending a claw.

"Denied," I quickly reply.

"Granted!" counters Billy, extending his hand towards Jackie, totally spellbound by the tall brunette wearing sheep's clothing.

The way the wagers work on a Formula 1 race are typical of any big sporting event. Gamblers can therefore choose to place bets on a wide range of outcomes such as *who will finish first* or *who will beat who* on the final grid.

There is also a wide array of exotic options for side bets available. For instance, you could bet on *which lap they will raise a yellow flag* or *which of the teams will make the shortest pit stop.*

That kind of stuff.

The odds and payout amounts are established and adjusted as the gamblers place their bets with the bookies before the race. Until the wager window closes. Then it's game on.

Of course, there are many websites where gamblers could also place their bets directly online. But you see, Monaco is kind of old school in that regard. There are always lots of dark interests maneuvering their way into town, particularly over the F1 weekend.

Lots of suitcases washing up from offshore. All filled with

money to be cleaned. In this town, if you want to bet big and under the table, especially with large sums in cash, it's best to go through a bookie like Casino Jackie.

Lots of suitcases
washing up from
offshore. All filled
with money
to be cleaned.

"So tell me Nolan. You dare come into my house..." starts Jackie.

It's a fucking casino.

"... sit at my table..."

Again, a casino.

"... and enjoy the complimentary drinks..."

She's unbelievable.

"... all of this without a kind word or a quick peck as you fly by?" complains Jackie.

I pick up a blue $200 token from my stack and throw it on the table mat in front of Jackie.

"Here, for your troubles," I say, hoping that would tame her hunger.

Jackie of course pockets the token, but we're not done yet. She quickly stands up, with blinking lucky sevens in her eyes. She grabs both Billy and I by the neck and twists our frail bodies in the direction of the TV screens. The local news is still looping the latest update about the upcoming qualifications and that *sick* pilot update.

"Now tell me my dear. It seems like you guys have found yourselves in some kind of a pickle. Haven't you?" she asks, fishing for fresh intel.

"We're still maneuvering."

"Tell me more?" asks Jackie.

"Marcus is gonna be fine," I tell her. "Doctors will give him a steroid shot in the cheek and he will be back on his feet in no time," I explain, trying to conceal the crisis with my usual nonchalance.

Meanwhile on the blackjack table, the dealer flips a Queen next to my four of clubs.

"Hum interesting," says Jackie before taking a pause. "It's just that... I wonder why they won't show Marcus on TV? You know what I mean. Why not show us the classic scene? A poor pilot lying in a hospital bed with a thermometer and an IV stuck in his arm?"

Jackie is many things but not an idiot.

"I find it a little bit *strange.* Isn't it? All of this seems a little bit odd in my book," she finally concludes.

I raise the bets and ask for another card. The dealer flips a nine of spades.

"Busted," says Jackie. "Now tell me Nolan, is there something going on here? Other than that *sick man narrative* they've been pushing all morning?"

Both the dealer, the old lady, my cousin, and Jackie stop and pause to look at me, waiting for a big reveal. Even the slot machines in the background seem to be holding on to their cherries.

"Listen Jackie, it is what it is. And that is that," I reply bluntly, leaving everyone on their appetite.

Jackie backs off and bites into a $100 chip. "Interesting. Because, that's not what *the streets* are saying."

Here we fucking go.

She whispers into my ear as the rest of the table leans forward. "I heard Marcus never made it out of that boat last night," Jackie says.

I jump from my seat. "Not here Jackie! Not now!" I tell her, as I start to shovel all of my chips into the front pocket of my hoodie.

"Let's get out of here, Billy!"

We both throw a $100 token over to the croupier, wink to the old lady who already forgot everything anyways, As we launch towards the exit, some of my chips spill down from my hoodie pocket and onto the floor. Patrons are rushing over to pick the tokens behind me. Call it trickle down economics.

I've read somewhere that casino carpets designs are devoid of straight lines on purpose in order to create a more efficient sense of blending in.

"Nolan! Wait a minute. There is a way we can work together," pleads Jackie.

We both turn around and Casino Jackie is standing there, hands on her hips, going full praying mantis mode like she's about to fuck us over, then gobble our heads.

"Go on," I tell her.

"You want to know what happened to your partner last night, right? And I need to clarify the landscape before the wagers start coming in this afternoon," Jackie explains.

Casino Jackie takes two steps forward. We take one step back. She has us now.

"There is a party going on upstairs in one of the high rollers suite, and there is a man up there that I would like you to meet. If somebody knows anything about Marcus' whereabouts, that would be him."

"A party? Jesus it's 11 a.m." I tell her.

"Hell yeah," shouts Billy.

"Well, the real party started last night," explains Jackie. "But from what I understand, it's rolling over today. Maybe this thing will catch a second breath once I throw you two cute logs into the fire. Come on! Aren't you even a little curious?"

And together, we make our way to the hotel elevator.

I fucking hate Casino Jackie.

16

The Never-Ending Party

The elevator doors open on a massive hotel suite filled with a bunch of colorful characters. Some are dancing on the couches, others are busy bending over a mirror coffee table.

There is enough blow on that table to feed a small village.

"Jackie!" shouts a man sitting on the couch and wearing only a red velvet bathrobe with the initials MM embroidered on his chest. The mountain of powder he sits in front looks like a science fair volcano. He invites us to move inside while he finishes lining up rails on the table with a plastic card.

Mickey Clarence Thomas. 186 cm. Needs to wear glasses.

That's what the driver license said.

"Gentlemen, that's Mickey Mouse," says Jackie.

The man springs up.

"And I see you brought us refreshments!" Mickey says, taking a good look at me. His eyes are still visible behind some yellow tinted sunglasses. He is scanning my body features from head to toes.

There is enough
blow on that table to
feed a small village.

"And not just an average Red Label, I see! What's your name son, Johnny Walker?" asks Mickey.

"I'm Nolan, and that's my cousin Billy," I reply.

"Oh! Yes, yes. The soapbox racer. Apologies, it's been a long night." He adjusts the sunglasses that keep on slipping down his sweaty nose, while recalibrating with a short sniffle.

"Why do they call you Mickey Mouse?" bluntly asks Billy, much entertained by this new flamboyant character.

"Because he's a sneaky little rat," answers Jackie.

Mickey laughs, displaying good sportsmanship.

"Because I have ears all over town," explains Mickey.

The host moves forward to properly greet us with a mafia kiss on both cheeks, then dances his index finger in front of my face like a magic wand.

"You my friend, you!" Mickey turns around and scoops up a vintage camera on the sofa and wraps the strap around his neck.

Meanwhile Billy is already helping himself over the coffee table.

"Sorry about my cousin, he has no table manners," I tell Mickey.

"I see. One snowflake and all the puffy coats come out!" he replies.

More dreams crushed into a fine powder.

"I heard you are doing pretty well for yourself. All of that money, and fame! Spinning around and around on the silver track." He dusts off my shoulders and raises up my chin like a show dog. "And good genes, too."

"Can't complain," I reply, with no idea where this is going.

Mickey Mouse raises the camera to my face.

"Now say *cheese*!" and we hear a snap. Mickey turns around and waltzes back to join two models still grooving on the sofa.

"Hey, what's the point of being rich if you're *not young*? Am I right?" states Mickey with his arm now wrapped around one of the models.

He's right.

"When I die, you can throw away all of my money from the tallest building, for all I care," I explain to Mickey and the rest of the court.

"When I die, I want you to fly my casket on top of a 747," says Billy after a jumbo line. "Like a fucking space shuttle."

Jolted up, his bathrobe open, Mickey Mouse twists towards the girls on the couch.

"Ladies, say cheese!"

"Cheeeeeese!" and the flash goes off again. Another snap.

I lean towards Casino Jackie, "How old are these girls?"

"They're okay. Mickey doesn't like green bananas," she explains.

"Now which one of you wants to see my dark room?" asks Mickey, holding the camera. "I'll let you play with the chemicals."

"Hold on, Mickey. Nolan here has some questions for you," interrupts Jackie.

Mickey Mouse jumps back on the floor. Focused.

"A little *quiz?*" asks Mickey, moving closer, still looking at me over the frame of his sunglasses. Sweaty forehead.

"My partner Marcus, the champion. He... *disappeared* last night. Would you know anything about that?" I ask him, slowly accepting that sooner or later, the cat will be out of the bag anyways.

"Hum. No luck my friend. For all I know, we've been locked up in here for the last 24 hours. The casino floor is kinda lava," explains Mickey, scooping a little bump with his *pinky* nail from the coffee table volcano.

"And what about a woman named Natalia?" I quiz again. "Blonde, sophisticated, and smoking long cigarettes."

Mickey's face suddenly lights up. "Oh you've met Natalia!"

"The local architect, yes. You happen to know her?" I inquire naively.

"Architect? You mean the *actress*, right?" he replies, with emphasis on the word 'actress' that he puts in air quotes with his fingers. "Natalia. Slender blonde, foreign accent?"

My lovely spy.

"She's a good friend of ours, yes indeed. She actually called me yesterday and said she was staying in town for a gig. Hired to *entertain* some VIP or something..."

My heart suddenly twisted and stopped inside my chest, looking for an exit.

Mickey must have understood from the look on my face.

"Oh dear... I'm so sorry."

17

Staring at the Sea

I shouldn't have listened to the songs of the sirens.

With my feet in the sand, I'm staring at the water in the distance.

The sea usually has something to tell me, but this time, nothing.

Just wave after wave. Going through the motions.

Everything so *choreographed*.

Seems like I fell victim to some kind of conspiracy.

But for *what*? And from *whom* exactly?

At least when you get killed by the secret services, they ultimately give you an odd sense of satisfaction in the end. They pull the trigger, the lights go out, and the black birds fly off.

And at that very last second, you finally know.
You know that you were right all along.

My phone is ringing, and it's Céline calling.

"Nolan, where the *hell* are you? Qualifications start now."

"I'm on my way," I reassure her.

Oh Captain, please strap me on that rocket.

I need to go fast.

Real fucking fast.

18

Qualifications

Walking through the paddocks, I pass between the different teams preparing to launch onto the circuit. Everyone takes a moment to stare at me as I walk by. They're probably wondering what's my game plan, now that Marcus is gone.

Now that I have to race this thing alone.

I carefully tuck the ankle bracelet inside of my jumpsuit, not to spark any suspicions.

Earlier on, I left cousin Billy at the casino like some sort of deposit. Now I can better focus on what matters the most right now: scoring the best possible time on the circuit.

To my right, I walk past Wallace "The Frenchman," as he slides into the cockpit of his blue car. He gives me a wink as we make eye contact in slow motion. Legend has it that his mom used to go jogging with him strapped in a stroller, just so he could get used to speed from a very young age.

To my left is the new Chinese young gun being zipped up, while another team member feeds him lunch through a straw in the crack of his helmet. His marketing team bought a giant billboard near the airport to feature him and his partner with the caption: *Days of the Dragons*. They might not be the fastest team, but they have +3 fearlessness.

Further down the alley, I walk past *Old McCallister*, a fading star now barely hanging on to his career. Some young bimbo, half his age gives him a good luck kiss before he locks his green helmet on.

Most losers fall back on trophy wives.

The mayor is here too, and with some pretty young thing of his own under his arm. She looks like a professional though. Later this afternoon, he's probably gonna give her that citizen cane.

Most losers fall back on trophy wives.

Finally, I reach my home base where everyone from our team awaits my arrival. I throw my phone to Céline, and the Captain throws back my helmet.

"To the moon, Nolan," he simply says.

As I slide into the rocket, I give one last look at the second car placed under a blanket next to me. The crew has prepared everything in case Marcus would show up last minute in some sort of Han Solo fashion to save the day. But no sign of him anywhere.

The mechanics finally clip the roll bar over my head.

My full metal jacket.

"Where are you Marcus?" I whisper at the empty red car parked next to mine. "Are you up there, playing golf with the ghost of your dead father? Maybe when I become a ghost too, we will finally play Pebble Beach together?"

Time to focus.

All strapped up, I'm waiting for the signal.

The way qualifications work in Formula 1 is quite simple.

Small batches of pilots will launch onto the circuit over three sessions of 20 minutes called Q1, Q2 and Q3. At the end of each of the sessions, the slowest pilots get recouped from the pole.

Overall, all pilots drive as fast as they can in an attempt to establish the best lap time possible on the circuit. These times will ultimately establish the final line up on the starting grid for the race tomorrow.

Quick fact: the record time for the fastest lap on the Monaco circuit during qualifications is 1.13.556 and was scored by Sebastian Vettel.

In my helmet, The Captain clears me for take-off. "To the fucking moon, Nolan."

I smash down the throttle, and everything becomes clear again.

19

The Sting

Q1 was easy.

We punched fast enough on the clock to escape the first tranche of pilots to fall off.

Now the real fun and games begin. The promise of the premise.

The crew puts up four brand new sneakers on my feet in less than four seconds before I zoom out of the pits, starting my second session.

The best lap time so far was scored by *The Frenchmen* at 1.15.789, but I know he's just sparring for now. We should expect him to shave another second over Q2.

The Monaco circuit design puts a long tunnel about halfway into the lap. Which is always a little tricky.

After spending three seconds in the dark, pilots burst out on the other side where the eyes will have to adjust again for daylight over a second or so. And trust me, a lot of things can happen within that second when you are driving the fastest car in the world.

Every time I'm swallowed into the tunnel, I'm reminded of the air capsules that the Wall Street brokers use to send the money orders up to the accounting floor.

This time, I'm the fucking money.

Passing through the checkered line once again, Céline updates me on my time. "You just punched 1.15.004 Nolan. You can do better than that."

You bet.

Now approaching the L-shaped turn along the harbor, I spot more and more spectators filling up the stands. I give a little more trust, and my car engine roars like a bat out of hell over the straight line.

Wake up, *motherfuckers.*

Back in the days, there was no security fence along the harbor. Sooner or later, someone was bound to end up in the water. Modern day safety in Formula 1 has prevented such a peril, but decades ago, Australian driver Paul Hawkins nosedived in the Mediterranean on lap 79th. He was quickly able to escape his sinking Lotus car and swim back safely ashore. He was greeted by his mocking mechanics who later attached a lifebuoy to his retrieved car with the moniker "Swimming Kangaroo."

Now exiting the hairpin curve, I quickly catch up with another pilot, my nose already stuck up his tail feathers.

In the rule book, overtaking is not permitted during qualifications, unless a driver is lapped due to mechanical problems. Today, pilots are only trying to beat the clock.

"Captain, it's the Mexican stalling me," I send over the radio.

"Easy cowboy, don't try anything stupid."

"But he's blocking the way! Looks like he's having troubles with a back tire or something. Do I have permission to pass, sir?"

"Go for it," clears the Captain.

Giving the steering wheel a sharp right, I squeeze on the inside lane between the Mexican's car and the curb. Unfortunately, he doesn't get to see me in time and contact is made. We scratch off some paint, sending sparks flying.

"Jesus Nolan, you're gonna cost me another leg!" screams the Captain. "All the monitors are blinking red."

"It's nothing, sir. It's nothing. Just a little kiss," I reassure the team over the radio.

Then I push on the gas, and the Mexican disappears as fast as he came. That lap is useless though, so I go for another round. Hitting the Saint-Devote turn, the Beau Rivage seawall, the Casino Square, then negotiate both Mirabeau turns, the Grand Hotel hairpin through Le Portier, under the Tunnel and finally pass the swimming pool complex to cross the checkered line once again.

"You just broke 1.14," says Céline on the radio. Behind her, I can hear the engineers and mechanics cheering at the clock.

"Keep it up, thunder," shouts the Captain.

That's very good. This means I probably secured a top 5 spot on the starting grid already.

"Nolan, you're not alone. The Frenchmen also broke the clock right before you," says Céline, halting celebrations.

Fucking douchebaguette.

And here comes the tunnel again. Three seconds of darkness before I flush out on the other side.

But all of a sudden, I hear a *clunk* within the fuselage and all of my instruments go dark.

Then my engine completely shuts down.

The car slows down on the track and grinds to a full stop.

"What the *hell* is going on, Nolan?" asks the Captain.

"No fucking idea, sir! Nothing is responding anymore!" I shout in my helmet, while repeatedly stabbing the start button. Yet nothing happens.

The lobster was cooked before it could smell the garlic.

"Try the manual restart," orders The Captain again.

The engine remains cold. The wheel is totally stiff.

"It doesn't work. Nothing works Captain!"

That car is dead.

It's like I was... *stung.*

20

No Go

Right after my car died on the circuit, I had to run up the remaining half a mile on the racetrack to find my way back into the pits. All the while, the stewards waved the yellow flag, and the crowds in the stands cheered as if a gladiator had just escaped the lion's jaw.

Once inside the hangar, I throw my helmet against the wall.

Then I throw a chair. Then I flip a table, smashing a bunch of keyboards in the process.

"Calm down, Nolan!" shouts Céline.

"Fucking electronics," I tell her.

The mechanics all stand still. One actually holds a fire extinguisher.

"Easy on the milkshake, brother," I warn him.

Then I turn to the Captain. "What the hell happened out there?"

"We don't know yet. We lost signal on all the sensors as well," the chief engineer explains.

Catching a breath, I turn to look at the second car still sleeping under the blanket. A spare chance.

"Gimme the keys," I ask.

"Nolan!" interferes Céline.

"Gimme the goddamn keys! I need to show them what I can do!"

"Nolan, I have management on the line..." she continues.

"Fuck these crows, they're not even here!" I shrug.

I swiftly pull the covers off Marcus' car, revealing the second red machine, intact and ready to go.

"That car is our only chance left Nolan," declares the Captain. "We need to assess and understand what just happened before we can send you back out there."

"Plus, management says it's a *no go*," confirms Céline. "I'm sorry Nolan."

I throw another chair at the wall.

21

Just Me and Mr. Croc

I'm drifting on an inflatable crocodile in the middle of the pool with a bottle of Canadian Club laying on my chest. I've locked all the doors of the villa and told the maids they could have the rest of the day off.

Finally, it's just me and Mr. Croc.

Through the bay window of the living room, I can clearly see that the local news spins over and over my disappointing performance of this afternoon on the racetrack. Someone also leaked a video of me breaking up stuff in the hangar. Such a pitiful scene to watch, streamed in a loop.

Pilot melts down on Monaco circuit, the title reads.

What a shame. I choose to swallow my pride with yet another sip of the bottle.

When it's no longer about the money, everything else is on the table.

I call Billy to know what's up, and he picks up on the first ring.

"Hey cousin, sorry about the *quals*. You okay?" he asks.

"Where are you right now?" I reply.
"Still at Mickey's. Still riding the slopes!" he says. I can hear the party still evolving in the background. They're gonna punch through the day. Like a fucking telethon. Except there are no more kids to save.

"Okay listen to me Billy, grab some of that blow to go, would you? And come meet me at the villa ASAP. We need to go somewhere," I tell him, with no further explanations. A good soldier should know when to rally.

I hang up and resume my lonely drifting.

About the qualifications. Something is not right. For a *techy* car like that to shut down instantly? With no flames or anything? You gotta wonder.

My right leg is trailing underwater to keep the black ankle bracelet soaked, otherwise this thing turns burning hot under the mid-afternoon sun.

Could this be an act of sabotage coming from someone inside my team? Someone who doesn't want me to replace Marcus as the top dog? I mean, I was not even asking for this in the first place. Deep down, we all know I wasn't quite ready.

Another sip. My eyes sweep in the direction of the empty pool house.

And what about Natalia? My lovely spy.

If this is all an elaborate plot against me, what could be the role of Natalia? I mean, other than being a pure distraction. Something bright enough to steer my attention away from the evil hands at work in the shadows.

Shiny things can fool even the smartest birds.

And what about Angelo and his brother? Clearly, they have something to do with the disappearance of Marcus. But what would be their motive here? Why screw around with two race car drivers in town just for a weekend? And don't we bring good business to town? That doesn't make any sense.

There are too many moving parts. I feel outnumbered. Marcus would know what to do. He always did. I try to gobble all the puzzle pieces with another sip from the now half-empty bottle.

We all wake up sober every morning, so it's kind of a fair game. It's just a little later during the day that things get complicated.

We all wake up sober every morning, so it's kind of a fair game.

All of sudden, the violent blades of the chopper are cutting through my obscure thoughts. I've locked all of the doors, plus the front gates and activated the electric fences. I never thought that someone would dare to violate my airspace.

My phone is ringing, and it's Billy, screaming.

"Nolan, move the garden furniture!"

Oh shit, he's gonna land on the grass. I swiftly eject from Mr. Croc and commando my way onto the lawn where I push aside all of the tables and chairs to make room for some improvised landing zone.

The chopper touches the grass, and the rotor stops.

Billy gets out, a pinch of white powder still under his nose.

"What's up cousin! Ready for some heli-skiing?"

Oh Billy. My white savior.

22

Special Delivery

Billy has drawn the map of the Monaco racetrack with white lines on the table, and I'm going full clip into the hairpin with one giant streak.

We synchronize.

"Whoa, this stuff is way better," I tell my cousin.

"Right? Feels like we're moving up the river with this batch," Billy says. "We're definitely cutting off some middleman going through Mickey."

"Pure shores ahead, baby."

"Now tell me Nolan, what is your plan exactly?"

Before I can spit out an answer, the front gate of our compound buzzes.

"Hold on," I tell my cousin, as I make my way towards the intercom on the wall and push the button that speaks the front gate language.

"Hello?" I ask inquisitively.

"Special delivery for Mr. Nolan," the voice says.

I don't say anything back and just look at my cousin who's now hiding under a table. Meanwhile on the security monitor above the intercom, we can see some delivery guy holding a small package. A yellow box.

"What do we do now?" I whisper. "Could be a trap."

"One *hundred* percent," whispers Billy.

The intercom asks again. "Hello? Special delivery for Mr. Nolan?"

"Go get it, Billy."

"Fuck no. *You* go get it."

I press the button again. "Hum yes, leave the package at the gate. We'll send someone. And thank you, kind sir."

Billy now sports a scuba mask and some oven mitts that he found in the kitchen.

"The enemy is at the gate."

"How could anyone know we're bunkered in here?" I wonder out loud.

The front gate buzzes again.

"Are you fucking kidding me?" says Billy

So much for being alone.

In the camera monitor, this time we see Céline, probably wondering why she can't access the villa with her clicker. The intercom speaks first. "Nolan, are you here?" Céline asks. "And why is everything locked? Did you change the codes or something?"

"I don't know, maybe? Tell us which side are you *on* Céline?" I ask, releasing the button of the intercom. Billy and I brace ourselves for a tough round of negotiations.

"What?" she asks. "There are no sides Nolan."

Billy covers the microphone of the intercom with the oven mitt.

"She could help," he says, pointing at the yellow box waiting in front of the gate next to her.

"All right, all right. Come in. And bring that package inside. Would you?"

We buzz her in. Doesn't mean I look over the fact that she sided with management earlier on today. Politics.

Céline, who was just cleared for access into our secret hideout, now stands in the kitchen with the yellow package in her hands. She stares at Billy still sporting the scuba mask in order to face any possible threat of Anthrax, or even worse.

"You guys are as high as the space station, aren't you?"

"We're just gliding," goes Billy.

Céline puts the yellow box in the middle of the kitchen island, and we all stand around it for a minute, before I finally take the lead and rip open the package.

You guys are high
as the space station.

Inside, we are surprised to find my old G-Shock watch. The one I had given to Marcus last night before he disappeared.

Next to it inside the box, lies a magnetic room key card from the Monte Carlo Casino & Hotel.

Finally, we find a handwritten note that says HAPPY BIRTHDAY NOLAN.

23

What Are the Odds?

The helicopter is bound for the Casino. If there's no traffic, we're gonna land on top. I'm turning and turning that magnetic card in my hand, but there's no room number on it. Nothing.

"I don't get it," I mutter. My thoughts circulate the whole cabin on the closed-circuit headphones we're all wearing.

"By the way, happy birthday cousin!" says Billy. "I didn't know it was coming up already. Where did we go last year? Was it Tulum?"

"Tulum was six months ago, and no, it's not my birthday," I tell him.

"You think the package comes from Marcus?" asks Céline. "Maybe they got him trapped somewhere. Maybe he's trying to send you a coded message."

"What is the message?" I ask to the cabin.

"We need to check with the front desk at the hotel. It's the only way to figure which room the key opens," explains Céline, contouring the early stage of a plan. She digs up whatever is left from the plastic tube Billy brought on board and sharpens up her senses.

She synchronizes.

"We're gonna need more of that," says Billy.

"This stuff is good," confirms Céline. "Super soft."

"While you guys take care of the front desk mission, I will swing by Mickey Mouse's PH. Collect more samples from the mouth of the volcano," says Billy.

"Mickey Mouse?" Asks Céline, intrigued.

"Oh, it's a long story," I shrug off.

"Hey, while we're all sitting here, I was wondering... Who's the real boss between the two of you?" goes Billy, looking for trouble again.

Céline and I exchange a brief professional look.

"Technically we all work for management," answers Céline. "And management works for the investors."

She's good.

"Hey, I'm an investor!" says my cousin, acting cute.

Céline suddenly slides the helicopter door wide open and points at the void below. "Do you feel like flying down the rest of the way Billy?"

"Okay relax, Scarface!" he says, holding on tight to his seat belt.

The chopper is now flying over the casino in a holding pattern, waiting for the authorization to land. I can't imagine the shit show we'll have to face going through that hotel lobby, now that my face has been blasted all over local TV for the past couple of hours. All of the questions and the paparazzi.

Plus, it's only 3 o'clock, and half of this town is already piss-drunk. That includes us.

We make a landing.

It's only 3 o'clock, and
half of this town is
already piss-drunk.

That includes us.

Down the elevator and into the lobby, all of the animals are on the loose.

"Oh fuck me, here we go again," I warn Céline and Billy as soon as I spot Casino Jackie walking straight in our direction.

"Nolan! My little spring chicken! Are you ready to lay down those golden eggs?" Jackie asks, moving more air with her overcoat than the chopper did a minute earlier.

Jackie wraps Billy and I by the shoulders with her long arms and walks us slowly amid a buzzing floor of slot machines operating in full swing.

Céline is strolling right behind us, a little bemused by the new fauna she just discovered.

"Tell me, Nolan, it's a nice little surprise you pulled off on qualifications this afternoon. The breakdown, the running on the tracks. Breaking up stuff in the hangar," Jackie says.

"It wasn't planned at all," I tell her.

Céline catches up to us. "Hey, is there an option to turn off the commentary on this one?" she asks, hinting at Casino Jackie.

But Jackie keeps up with her routine.

"Planned or not my friends, the bets are now rolling in like crazy," she confesses.

"What *kind* of bets?" I ask.

"Well, there is one type of wager in particular..." Jackie starts. "People are betting against you, Nolan."

"Against *me*? Why?" I ask, this time a little confused.

"Well, after what happened during qualifications, some big wallets are betting that you will *not* finish the race. That your team is doomed for the weekend. At the moment, odds are looking about 20 to 1".

"They are shorting you!" says Billy.

"Oh no, that's really bad," I tell Jackie.

"Depending for who!" she counters. "When it comes to me, I just keep the house in order."

Céline throws a monkey wrench into our little chat and calls for order. "Boys, we're on a mission here. Chop chop," she claps, breaking up the group.

"See you later, my minions!" shouts Jackie with a swift twist of her overcoat, propelling herself further down into the abyss of the casino floor.

Are people really betting against *me*?

Feels like they're *shorting* me. Not hard to believe. But I didn't ask for any of this shit. Yesterday I was coasting behind Marcus.

And yet, today I find myself on the front seat, dealing with all of the splish and the splashes.

Billy splits and goes to the elevator.

Céline and I beach at the front desk where she snaps her fingers at the clerk. I try to stay low-key and remain at an angle to avoid being fully identified. She shows the magnetic card to the guy.

"Listen, our dad booked the room this morning, and my dumb brother here totally forgot the room number. Care to refresh our memory?" she asks.

"Happy to help! What is the *name* on the register?" asks the clerk, in the signature pretend altruism proper to hotel staff.

"Oh, it's kinda confidential," says Céline, trying a wink and a crisp $50 bill she slides slowly on the counter.

"I can't check the computer without a name, ma'am. If you found that card on the floor, you can leave it safely with us. We'll wait for the rightful owner to claim it."

Céline plucks back the cash from the clerk's hand, along with the key card.

"Never mind, kiddo."

We both pull up our sunglasses at the same time and perform a dash towards the exit. The afternoon sun is very bright and well hung. Billy should be back down in a minute with some reinforcements.

As we reach the sidewalk, an impromptu white van circles the roundabout in front of the Casino entrance and screeches to a halt right in front of us.

The panel door slides wide open, and three goons jump outside.

Before we can do anything, one of the men puts a black hood over Céline's head and shovels her inside the van.

Then it fades to black for me too.

24

Kidnapped

I've been breathing through a potato sack for the past twenty minutes. Céline and I are sitting side by side on plastic folding chairs.

"Hey, while we're here, how did that go with the Royal Envoy last night? Got lucky?" I ask Céline.

"I'm afraid he rather has an acquired taste for altar boys," she explains.

"Oh. I kinda see it now. You think you could *flip* him?"

"Given enough time? Maybe," she simply says.

Céline and I had a couple of close calls in the past. We never hooked up or anything, but let's say that I understand her appeal. It's just that I feel we are way more efficient as friends for now.

One of the tough guys finally removes the black hoods from our heads. We both know where we are. We're back in the concrete jungle. We're back on the top floor of the Emerald Tower.

"Oh wow. Aggressive marketing guys. I'm impressed," shouts Céline. "But we told you, we're not in the market for a seven bedroom condo sharing gym amenities with Gaddafi's nephew."

There's an empty table in front of us. They did not tie our hands or anything but we kinda get the message. We find ourselves surrounded with gorillas, pointing real pieces, no bananas.

The three men, who brought us here, now stand with their hands behind their backs, awaiting instructions from whoever is behind this lame stunt.

"Is this an episode of Shark Tank? Are you gonna pitch us your big invention now?" I ask the gorillas. But not a word. "Honestly guys, I would give you whatever the fuck you want right now for 10% of the gig, if that means we can get the hell out of here and swim back to the hotel."

"Regroup with our fellow dolphins," adds Céline.

It's always easy to tell apart the low life gangsters by the knockoff brands they are wearing. Shrunk up sweaters. Logos printed too big. Whenever you see a big catch by the DEA on the news, it's always POLO Ralph Lauren. You know, that stupid shirt with the big horse. Except they never made that shirt, you idiots.

We hear footsteps approaching on the concrete floor. Someone finally walks in.

"Angelo?" I ask, not so surprised.

"Ladies and gentlemen," he says, smiling. Looking fresh, I admit.

"You could have just called, you know?" says Céline.

"Are you for real?" I add.

"Oh, trust me, it's real," the evil developer says.

He removes his jacket and lays it on the chair in front of us, then rolls up his sleeves.

"Nolan, my friend, I apologize for the small inconvenience, but time is at the essence here. And I thought a busy woman like you, Céline, might appreciate the efficiency of this exchange."

"Go on," she says.

"I've organized this expedited meeting as a courtesy, since after all, you and Marcus are our dear guests in town this weekend," continues Angelo.

Céline is not having it.

"Oh, so this is a meeting now?" she asks, cranking up the attitude to a solid seven.

"What have you done to Marcus?" I ask, also getting agitated. But one of the gorillas is pressing down on my shoulders to keep me seated.

Evil characters like Angelo should only be allowed to exist on a specific island like the Komodos.

All very toxic.

"I'm afraid we have *nothing* to do with the disappearance of your partner. You can trust me on that," pledges Angelo, hands in his pocket.

"Trust you?" spits Céline. "Oh right. Says the guy who hires Blackwater just to book a conference room."

Evil characters like Angelo should only be allowed to exist on a specific island like the Komodos.

All very toxic.

"Okay, quiet now," waves Angelo. Regaining control of the room.

The developer reaches behind his back and pulls out a black gun from under his belt, and puts it on the table right in front of us.

The first time you see a gun during business hours is when you realize that you've drifted way too far from the cubicle.

"It may all come as a surprise to you right now, but it has become apparent that our mutual interests are very much aligned at the moment," explains Angelo, capturing our attention.

"Go on," I tell him, even though my eyes are still fixated on the black metal piece laying on the table.

"You see, at the time of your partner's disappearance, Marcus and I had some sort of an *arrangement*," details Angelo.

"An... *arrangement?*" I ask the crooked developer. "What type of arrangement are we talking about here?"

"It was regarding the race tomorrow." Angelo says. "Especially about *the outcome* of the race."

"You must be joking," says Céline, now laughing.

Angelo suddenly gets super mad and bangs on the table. The gun bounces a little closer.

"Year after year, all of you maggots fly into our town to plunder and do whatever you like," Angelo screams. "You come in this town like a wrecking ball. But trust me, this time, you'll be lucky if we even let you leave with the scraps."

He catches a breath. I think we all do.

"But now that the beloved champion has gone missing, I find myself in a rather embarrassing position," he continues.

"And so do we," calmly says Céline, trying to diffuse.

"What was *the arrangement?*" I ask again.

"Marcus agreed to lay down in the middle of the race. Retire without completing the event. Forfeiting the race all together."

"And then?" asks Céline.

"And then, me and my associates would rack a colossal wager placed on his head. For his troubles, we had agreed to pay Marcus two million dollars."

Céline and I pause for a moment. That's a lot to take in right now.

This is hardly making any sense. Why would Marcus pull such a grotesque stunt in order to rack up a few more millions? The man is already rich as fuck.

But this question is for another time. I focus my attention back to Angelo. There's something else I need to know.

"So now I understand that you have something to do with the

sudden breakdown of my car during qualifications?" I ask him.

Angelo raises his chin.

"You can call that our insurance policy. In case Marcus wouldn't comply with our agreement. And I believe it's safe to say now, that our little test was successful," confesses the developer.

Unbelievable.

"Now given the turn of events, my associates and I are willing to extend the same offer to you Nolan. Two million, if you accept to lay down for us in the middle of the race."

"Accepting two million to *lay down*?" I ask.

"That's right. Otherwise, we will shoot you down Nolan. At least we are kind enough to let you forfeit on your own terms. You could simulate a crash, a pit stop malfunction, whatever. I don't care honestly! As long as you lay down and *don't* cross that finish line."

A pause.

"Go fuck yourself," I finally tell him.

"You've been warned, Nolan. We will shut you down again."

"Game on motherfuckers. You catch me if you can.

Angelo smirks. Fucking little weasel.

"Now you listen to me, and you listen to me good. I *will* finish that race, and you will lose all of your money," I tell Angelo and the gorillas.

"Yeah, you stupid prick. What you are doing here is totally wrong," piles on Céline.

She takes a moment to look around the room before she continues.

"And I bet that in less than five minutes, the cops are going to burst into this fucking place and take you down! Because you see, Nolan has a tracker on his ankle. The police totally know where we are right now."

Angelo starts laughing out loud with his back turned to us. Then he pivots in our direction, holding his phone in his hand.

"And tell me, how do you think we've found you?" he asks.

Angelo points to a red blinking dot on the map of his phone.

"Peekaboo, that's you!" he says.

So there it is. The big plot.

The brothers tried to rig the race in their favor to collect a wager. Except that their scheme went south as soon as Marcus disappeared. That means someone, somehow, canceled their evil plan.

Now what if I decide to take the deal? Will I disappear *too*?

One thing, for sure, is that we can't trust the Royal envoy anymore. He gave us away with that ankle bracelet. Fucking lizard rat.

Angelo circles back to the table, picks up the gun, and puts his suit jacket back on. He then reaches for the inside pocket.

"Oh and before we go..."

He throws a bunch of photographs and negatives in the middle of the table. All featuring Billy and I in the process of buying drugs at the back of the dry cleaner.

"Just a little *souvenir* from our friends at the police station," says Angelo. "Careful with that stuff Nolan. Wherever there's powder, there's a bullet nearby."

Angelo drops the mic then picks up the gun. We've been set up from the get-go. And now I guess we can't trust the cops either.

The developer and the gorillas walk away towards the elevator.

Now, there is one particular thing that doesn't make any sense to me. Why would Marcus accept such a petty deal?

25

Two Years Ago in Prague

When rich people die in a plane crash, all we find is their Amex Black.

Fortunately, nothing happened this time, and our direct flight with Lufthansa landed safely in one of the rare cities in Europe that was never bombed during the World Wars.

> When rich people
> die in a plane crash,
> all we find is their
> Amex Black.

Marcus and I opted for this little bromance trip together in an attempt to catch some fresh East European air halfway through the season. It is now our third-year racing together, therefore it deserved a little celebration.

I've never been to Prague before. Everything here is museum quality.

The castles, the cobblestone streets, and the gloomy canals depict a blueish gray town from which the good stories tend to emerge only at night.

The whole Poe aesthetic.

Forgotten names and tales of distant conquests are marked on some gravestones that no one comes to visit anymore. Many generations too far to relate. But here they are, still standing, respecting the decorum.

And always that damp fog shrouding the whole thing in more mystery.

We've landed last night but didn't catch much sleep since the lads staying in the next room kept throwing furniture into the walls while shouting Viking chants.

This morning (around noon) we obviously asked these idiots where in town we could secure that much fun for tonight. They've told us they've been chasing the Green Fairy. They said that they could take us somewhere off the books tonight, if we could keep a secret.

And that is why we are now trailing these two tall backpackers. Their Slavic names elude me once again. All on track for an introduction ritual with the Green Fairy in some underground pub they call The Grotto. Literally.

The four of us walk across the famous Charles Bridge which connects both banks of center Prague, better known as the old and new city. Even though everything looks equally old as shit.

Underneath the giant medieval stone arch bridge erected in the 15th century, the water is raging and probably freezing cold. The bridge is decorated by a continuous alley of thirty statues and reinforced by three bridge towers, projecting strong baroque vibes over our journey across.

"Can you imagine the number of bodies that were thrown from up here?" says Marcus, hypnotized by the violent currents breaking on the legs of the bridge and the icebreakers upstream.

"You ship them directly to Austria!" I add, standing on the side ledge to look down.

One of the lads throws an empty beer can overboard and it just disappears, swallowed whole and washed away into the white foam. Such an unforgiving city.

Here we are, Marcus and I, once again walking on the bridge between the haves and the haves not. The old and the new world coming together for the sake of a little entertainment.

Chasing the Green Fairy together.

The consumption of Absynth a.k.a. *La Fée Verte* a.k.a. The Green Fairy was banned in the US around 1912 because it was believed that the green spirit contained in the bottles was hallucinogenic and dangerous. I can understand the appeal. It has now since been reinstated and sold as a moderate, less potent version.

Now I believe Prague is where they keep the real stuff. Especially if you are about to treat yourself to something that is *off the menu,* as our dear Slovak guides did promise.

We've made it across the Bridge and beyond the fortifications of the old city. Which means more gargoyles, basically. More rusty chains rattling in the wind. More dark passages underneath 15th century archways.

Lots of tourists are massed at the foot of a giant clock tower.

"What are they doing?" I ask our Slovak guide.

"They are waiting for the clock to ring," he explains.

"Isn't it what we're all doing?" says Marcus.
The Slovaks make a left and begin to descend in one of those narrow archway entrances and of course, we follow. No way I'm staying outside alone. I'm pretty sure there are more ghosts per square mile here than anywhere else in the world. The stone passage is covered with moss and creeping vines. We begin to hear the reverberation of some music coming from further down.

We walk down the stone corridor, then push a rusty gate,

and finally spiral down another narrow stone staircase to find exactly what the postcard said: The Grotto Pub. An underground bar nestled in some medieval dungeon cave. An alcove of warmth amid a cold gray scale of a town.

"It is true what they say about East European women," I tell Marcus, hinting at the tall and good looking women smoking outside the entrance.

"Or maybe this town is just so goddamn cold that anything will do for a lost sailor strained on this forsaken rock."

We finally step inside The Grotto, nestled in some underground cellar.

At the end of the room, a giant fireplace with real fire and logs, breathes life into the whole cavernous hideout. There is a long wooden table on which the locals and a few lucky tourists like us are banging on with their fists, before chugging metal mugs of beer and mead, a concoction of fermented honey and water.

Humidity and sweat pearls on the rocky ceiling.

The stone bar made of a single slab along the right side wall is packed with rare spirits, aged whiskey bottles and burning candles. Years of compounding melting wax is stacked and dripping. But none of these trinkets glow and lure as brightly as the green elixir bottles lined up on the upper shelf carved directly into the bedrock.

The Green Fairy lives here.

As we make ourselves noticed by the staff, a beautiful woman wearing a brown cape motions the four of us to come sit at small round table in a dark corner. She lights up a candle and disappears towards the bar.

"You were here last night?" Marcus asks the Slovaks.

"Yes, she knows exactly what we want," the lad replies in broken English.

Behind him, a row of black and white closed-circuit televisions display different women dressed in provocative baroque nightgowns.

"What is this?" I ask our friends, pointing at the monitors.

"It's the menu," he replies.

"They are hookers," adds the other.

The brown cape woman circles back to our table and deposes a strange apparatus in the middle of the table. This is the fountain, used to release ice cold water in the absinthe goblet. A "louche" is created when iced water from the fountain is slowly dripped into the glass to mix with the liquor, releasing the aromatics. It also dictates the right rhythm for the ritual.

Between the water and the liquor, a sugar cube is placed on a spoon, which will slowly dissolve into the mix. Making the concoction a little more palatable for initiates like us.

The drip of the fountain gradually turns the solution into a milky green elixir in front of our eyes. A point of no return has been reached and the Slovaks don't seem to bother as they scoop the glasses and wet their beaks.

After several kisses of the Green Fairy, the flames of the fireplace begin to detour strange visions on the cellar walls. The whole soundscape is melting into a blur, the voices become distant, some of them muted. There is no fear though, only a warm sense of euphoria enveloping my whole being. Tucking me in.

We might not know much about our Slovak friends, and yet, our individual journeys are now connected through this joint ceremony. One for the memories.

This brief moment of introspective bliss is quickly interrupted by a commotion in the middle of the room. On the floor next to the long table, a man collapses and starts shaking like a leaf.

"We have a bacon man!" shouts Marcus, raising his glass over the table.

"Bacon-man!" both shout the Slovaks, imitating the gesture.

The staff and the brown cape women rush to attend to the fallen man, but after only a few minutes, the room quickly resumes to its orderly chaos. They must be used to it around here. Bad heroine can slip into the smallest cracks.

"I told you they had the good stuff," one of the lads mumbles.

"Hey, let's get some fresh air, shall we?" declares Marcus, standing up.

"You go, we stay here," says the lad.

Marcus and I move towards the exit, as we both realize how our faculties are impaired. In fact, it's way more visual than an actual body buzz. It's in the shapes and colors that reflect on the cavern walls. It's about what lurks in the shadows.

Murmurs.

"Let's get the fuck out of here!" says Marcus.

"What about *them?*" I ask.

"We know where they live, come on. This place gives me the creeps."

Outside on the street, everybody looks like they're selling something.

"Careful!" I shout.

A scooter zooms past the curb and almost runs over Marcus.

"They probably never heard of insurance over here," shrugs Marcus, pulling back the lapel of his overcoat.

Plus, only the assassins will wear a helmet.

The streets of Prague are totally overrun with scooters. Probably the fastest way to deliver the stolen organs. Laws appear to be more of a guideline around here.

We walk down the street and see people lining up in front of what seems to be a discotheque. One of those discotheques nothing good ever comes out. Yet outside, some cool kids are huddling like penguins. Two tall women in fur coats bypass the whole line and get inside with no fuss.

"Damn, those women were smoking hot. Something in the water, maybe?" I ask.

"Hey, the regime has been starving them for years, remember?" Marcus replies. "Let's go check it out."

There is something with people living in cold countries. Winter kinda makes you hopeful.

The discotheque is erected on the Old City bank of the river Vltava. A giant red neon sign is spanning across the building. "*The Karlovy Lazne,*" attempts Marcus.

"Oh, I've read about this place!" I tell him.

We immediately aim for the front of the line. A professional deformation, I guess. Luckily for us, the Nordic man with the black turtleneck guarding the door seems to recognize Marcus, and we're allowed to move through. See ya later, suckers.

The discotheque has five different floors. All boasting different music and vibes.

We're both wearing all black, so we sneak past the coat check.

We climb on the second floor where the DJ is blasting dance music in a non-ironic fashion, and we're drawn into the well. The Green Fairy hasn't totally worn off yet, so the lasers and the strobes hit straight past our defenses. Intermittent smoke machines reveal a sunken dance floor surrounded with a glass bridge where guests are also dancing head-to-head with the DJ. The floor is packed, two hundred kids maybe.

"It's a bit much," says Marcus. "Let's go up a level."

We climb on the third floor where the setup is a bit more casual, more linear. That's the floor where they play some *oldies.* There is a semi-circular section of booths and couches on the right, allowing guests to chill and order bottle service.

In the middle of the room sparks a checkered dance floor where the squares light up as the dancers step on them. The first guitar strokes of Twist and Shout set the room on fire, and all of a sudden, most of the beached whales on the couches flock back to the dance floor.

"Look, it's them," I tell Marcus, pointing at the two tall women dancing in the middle. Fur coats still on and wide open, flapping as they twist.

"They don't respect anything!" says Marcus, launching on the floor first.

We twist and we shout, slowly and cleverly shortening the distance between our two parties until we finally meet up at the center. Yellow, blue, and red squares blink under our feet. The room spins, and the minx coat of the redhead I'm courting keeps on sliding between my fingers like wet soap, providing more challenge and excitement to the hunt.

A few words are exchanged, and soon enough, we hit singularity.

We then let our bodies do the talking.

At about the third song into our act, I feel a tap on my shoulder. The redhead woman dancing on my arm goes, "uh oh."

When I turn around, a bald and very rough looking man stands three inches away from my face.

And he's not dancing.

"Hey what's going on here," shouts Marcus, pushing his way towards us. The rest of the dance floor quickly dissipates, except for two other ugly leather jackets closing in. We're obviously outnumbered. The two women back away, and I kinda feel some sort of disappointment in the way they abdicate and retract towards the side booths.

"You fuck off," says one of the baldies.

"We're just dancing here! Chill out," replies Marcus.

"Oh, you wanna dance?" adds the tough guy.

He lifts the flap of his undershirt, revealing a revolver tucked under his belt. His cronies are mirroring the same effect.

I believe it's a wrap. We bow down and get the fuck out of the discotheque. Not even glancing at the fur coats on the way out.

Back on the cold street, Marcus is not having it.

"Fucking cheaters!" he screams at the edifice.

"Calm down, we're kinda far from home Marcus."

"It's just not fair. We were having a good time, no? And these idiots are ugly as fuck," he adds.

Marcus then catches a breath and adjusts his jacket. Regaining his composure.

"I will never respect the cheaters."

26

Cut Loose

"That fucking weasel," says Céline in the elevator while on our way to Mickey Mouse's never-ending party, hoping that Billy is still waiting for us there.

"I told you from the beginning! At least now we both know what is what."

"Still, that doesn't help us at all. If Angelo doesn't have a clue about what happened to Marcus, who else is involved?" she asks.

Whoever is behind this plot got us swimming in the deep end now. And there are lots of gators in this pond. Ready to chew us up and spit out the Nikes.

"I'm sorry to ask, and I know he's family... But could Billy have anything to do with this?" asks Céline.

"Cousin Billy?" I ask her, my head corked.

"Yeah, I mean the timing is quite particular, don't you think? He shows up this weekend, unannounced."

"Come on, Céline. My cousin has the attention span of a mozzarella stick. No chance in hell he has the wits to come up with some elaborate scheme, let alone coordinate without making some stupid mistakes."

Céline smiles in acknowledgment.

My cousin has the attention span of a mozzarella stick.

"You know, his addiction is not the problem," she explains. "That's his excuse not to grow up. It keeps him day-to-day instead of having to plan for the future."

The elevator opens up and spits us back into the never-ending party. This place is like an airport lounge where nothing ever changes. Stuck in time. The air only cycled. Snacks replenished.

"Okay," says Céline at the view of slender girls dancing on the sofa, next to a mountain of pure blow. Jungle music and tam tam rhythms are tying up the whole scene together.

"That's the long story I was talking about," I tell her.

"Where the *fuck* did you go?" asks Billy, joining us along with Mickey.

"Brought me any new *flesh* offerings?" adds our host.

"We ran into Angelo and his gorillas," explains Céline. "He offered Nolan a large sum of cash to rig the race in their favor. I'm not fucking with you."

"Angelo *Tomassino*?" asks Mickey. "I'm surprised these *buffoons* still have any cash left in the piggy!"

"What do you mean?" asks Céline, perplexed.

"The Brothers are totally broke!" shouts Mickey, hands in the air. "They desperately need a cash infusion to complete the construction of the tower. And I've heard that their line of credit with The Royal Family has been maxed out."

Interesting.

"That would explain the erratic wager and the auction of their art assets over the weekend," I tell Céline and Billy, now both up to speed.

"And what about your meltdown on the racetrack?" asks my cousin. "Was it also their doing?"

"That's the part we quite don't understand yet. We need to

speak with the Captain," says Céline. "We know they *shot* Nolan down, we just have no idea how they did it."

I excuse myself and reach for the balcony while my phone is dialing up for the Captain. From up here I can see the paddocks and the circuit bustling with action. So close yet so far.

The Captain picks up.

"Yes, listen Captain. They are doing something with the cars," I tell him off the bat.

"They?" he questions.

"We don't know who, or what, and I don't have time to explain everything. But you guys need to look closely at the cars. Try to find something off. Something screwing up with the electronics or something. I'll call you later."

I walk back into the penthouse.

"We need to go back on that yacht," I tell Céline and Billy, now busy rolling up a piece of paper on the edge of Mount St. Helens.

Cliff notes.

"What about the hotel key card?" asks Billy.

"It's a dead end for now. The front desk won't help us," I explain. "But we could still sneak on the boat while it's tied up in the harbor. Let's try to figure out what happened last night when we heard the *splash*."

Céline points at my ankle monitor. "First thing first, we need to cut you loose from that thing, if we hope to sneak anywhere undetected."

Mickey goes into his makeshift darkroom and comes back with a sharp set of acetate cutters he uses on negatives. That should do it. In a swift upward slice, he cuts through the bracelet and hands it off to Céline like a dead tarantula.

"Let's put this evil thing into a cab. I'll pay the driver to circle around town. That should buy us enough time under the radar," plots Céline.

"What do you think we will find on that boat?" asks Billy.

"No idea. But we still need to know what happened to Marcus."

27

Sneaking Back on the Yacht

The three of us are looking at the Yacht sitting duck at the end of the pier.

"Any bright ideas now, about how we're gonna sneak aboard that thing?" asks Billy.

"By the front door," I reply. "It's Monaco. No one is stealing anything unless it's very big."

"Unless it's very small," continues Céline.

There is no in between.

Local movers busily unload art crates off the boat. No signs of Angelo or his security lurking around though.

"Look!" says Céline, pointing at the cleaning crew cart next to the boarding ramp.

"The good old cleaning crew heist, really?" I ask. "No way. It's so *cliché.*"

"And yet, that is why it's gonna work," she replies.

Five minutes later, we push a cleaning cart up the ramp, wearing matching white polo shirts. Céline passes on the vacuum to Billy. "You're good at *blowing dust,* am I right? Come with me upstairs. Nolan, you search this deck, would you?"

"Roger that."

Up on the outside deck, I circle around the boat towards where the *splash* came from last night. I keep thinking about what Mickey told us earlier regarding the Brothers. The fact that they were totally broke. The fact that they needed a quick infusion of cash in order to save their crumbling empire.

It's usually when you need to win that you ultimately lose.

One floor above the cabin where Natalia and I made out before the incident, I inspect the railings and the wooden deck. Looking for any traces of struggle or maybe a fight. But nothing.

The white shiny paint of the hull on the other side of the railing is clean all the way down to the water. There's no trace of anyone sliding down or holding on for his life.

Further along the deck, there is a bunch of patio furniture, some plants and coffee tables. Everything is in mint condition.

Wait a minute.

There is a row of long chairs aligned and facing towards the water. Three chairs in total, but clearly, it seems like there was a fourth one aligned right there at the end. I can perfectly see how the sun and the salty breeze has demarcated the contour of a fourth heavy long chair on the teak deck.

Could someone have thrown that chair overboard, creating a *splash?*

"Hey Nolan, come over here!" shouts Billy in a whispered voice coming from the staircase below.

I slide down and circle back on the main deck to enter the belly of the whale, where I find my cousin standing in front of two giant French doors that he pushes open, revealing a massive study. The whole room is detailed with warm essences of forbidden mahogany wood.

"That must be Angelo's office."

The circular room is filled with the usual villain memorabilia: a giant terrestrial globe, crossed elephant tusks on the wall, a vintage spyglass on a stand and bookshelves filled with leather tomes no one ever touches. I wouldn't be surprised to find Machiavelli in there.

"This place is huge," says Billy.

Bigger cage, bigger lions.

Behind the desk is perched a life-size marble bust of Com-
modus, the evil gladiator emperor. You gotta admire Angelo
for taking his cosplay very seriously. Does he know that it's
ultimately Narcissus that will kill him in the end?

Bigger cage,
bigger lions.

On the massive desk, in the center of the room, are scattered
floor samples, construction plans, and stacks of suppliers'
invoices. Most of them are probably overdue.

All of this and *one yellow package.*

A yellow package similar to the special delivery we received
earlier at the villa. Same handwriting, same size, and all.

"Billy, look." I point to the teared open package.

"That goddamn thing again!"

No fear this time, the box is already open. Empty.
Someone has been sending packages to both Angelo and me.

Someone is playing with us.

"Look what else I just found! Say hello to my little friend." says

Billy, this time jolly and waving a silver gun in the air.

A silver gun yet, no silver bullet.

"Take it." I tell him. "We might need it later. Let's get out of here."

As we sneak outside Angelo's office, we walk through the main living room where I quickly stop in my tracks. Something on the wall is missing.

"The painting, it's missing," I tell Billy.

"So what? They probably sold it at the auction this morning. Who cares? Come on, Nolan, we gotta move!"

The Sting. I remember now.

The poison and the antidote, said the old man the moment we were both standing exactly here last night, during the party. It was right before the splash. Right before Marcus disappeared from the radar.

"Nolan!" screams Céline from the outside deck. "We're moving!"

"What?" I shout back.

"The boat! We're leaving dock!"

"Jesus, I thought we were alone in here! Let's *fucking* go, Billy."

We all make a run to the back of the boat, but it's too late. The anchor is up, and the ramp is gone. The Yacht drifts toward the mouth of the marina. No one aboard seems to have noticed us yet, but I figure it's just a matter of time. The boat is rapidly gaining speed.

"What do we do now?" asks Billy, in a hurry.

"Just jump!" says Céline, launching herself first into the white foam at the back of the stern.

Billy and I follow. And once we all emerge out of the water, we both start paddling back towards the shore.

"Unbelievable!" screams Céline.

"We were searching Angelo's office. We didn't feel anything moving at all!"explains Billy, swimming and doing his best to keep the silver gun above the water.

"Found anything *else* in there?" asks Céline.

"Turns out someone has been sending a yellow package to Angelo as well," I debrief her, struggling with my drenched clothes.

We decide to ditch the polo shirts and the khakis to ease the swim.

Then Céline realizes something.

"Oh no! You gotta be fucking kidding me!" she screams, slapping the water around her. Imploring the gods up in the air or something.

"What *now* Céline?" I ask her.

"The magnetic hotel key. It was inside my vest... in the cart... on the yacht."

She lets herself sink.

"Happy fucking birthday, cousin!"

28

One Cruel Frame

A lot of things can happen within one frame.

You can have your heart broken for instance.

The three of us were handed out blue mechanics overalls to cover our wet underwear after we finally made it into the hangar. It's a blue-collar day, I suppose.

We stand in front of the controls and monitoring panel made of six screens. The Captain is busy toggling and rewinding the video footage from one camera in particular.

My dashboard camera.

At super high speed, this camera keeps chomping up the circuit and in a time lapse. At the bottom right of the screen are indicated the lap numbers during the qualifications session.

The captain rewinds the footage up to the point I'm about to exit the tunnel. Right before my car had unexpectedly shut down. We find ourselves looking at the middle section of the dark tunnel. The captain finally freezes the image on the screen.

"Look, over here," he says, pointing at the corner of the monitor.

Since the car was moving pretty fast and the footage was captured in low light, everything on the screen is kinda blurry except for one frame.

One cruel frame.

"That's how they did it," declares the Captain. "Whoever is standing there in that picture, that's how they shot you down Nolan."

The single frozen frame shows a slender figure wearing a black jumpsuit and a black full face motorcycle helmet.

The dark figure is pictured holding a futuristic looking device that resembles a rocket launcher. The design is bulky and looks quite heavy. Something I've never seen before. The device is made of a long chamber on which a black tube is mounted on the end. The whole thing reminds me more of a police radar gun than an actual weapon.

"A fucking bazooka?" I ask the Captain.

"That's nice," says Billy.

"Yeah, not nice," the Captain replies. "That thing is a ray gun."

"A *ray* gun?" I ask, intrigued.

"Instead of bullets, that canon shoots an electromagnetic pulse, which if aimed correctly at the target, has the power to disable any electronics onboard."

"So it's an EMP? Like in video games, am I right?" asks Billy.

"That's right. Except this time, shit is real," confirms the Captain. "This is military grade equipment guys. Something the army usually employs to disable radar towers and surveillance drones in the desert."

Part of me is half impressed and half puzzled at such a simple tactic.

"Wait, how many shots can this thing fire before recharging?" I quiz the Captain. "I mean, we're all driving pretty fast in the tunnel. That window of opportunity must be pretty small."

"At full power, I'd say the shooter has one, maybe two chances to shoot you down. We've scanned the tapes, and it's the only time we see the shooter in action on the footage," explains the chief engineer.

I hunch over the monitor and stare closely at the slender and semi-blurred figure pointing the ray gun towards the racetrack. A magnetic bazooka. Unbelievable.

"What do you wanna do with this?" asks the Captain. "Should we alert the authorities?"

"You mean the Formula 1 committee? Fuck that, they're the most corrupt of them all. No, I say we deal with this shit ourselves."

Getting a grip on the toggle wheel of the video console, I slightly turn the control mallet up and down, animating the slender character on the screen, frame by frame. Impossible to get a totally clear picture though.

"Who *are* you?" I whisper at the screen.

It's only when the dark figure dances from the second to the third frame, that I notice something flickering at the back of the motorcycle helmet.

A wick of blond hair.

29

A Fortress of Secrets

It's getting dark now.

After our post-mortem meeting with the Captain, regarding the lone shooter, I felt I needed a breather. Therefore, I offered a little cash incentive to the young skipper of the speedboat, and I asked him to take us into the bay. Simulating an escape from the Fortress.

Céline has retired back to the villa to deal with management, so I figured it was my turn babysitting. Now it's just me, Billy, and the young skipper, who is more than happy to collect a fare equivalent to a charter flight.

From here, the lure of the glowing Fortress is quite appealing.

Almost harmless. The joyful colors of a controlled burn to be admired at a distance. Except you and I both know that just a cigar thrown in the right place would suffice to blow up this rock at any moment.

Tonight, the whole town is burning to know what's gonna happen tomorrow.

The water is calm, and when the skipper turns off the engine to let us adrift, we can hear the distant bass lines of the many beach bars and private yacht parties lining up the shore.

The whole town is
burning to know
what's gonna
happen tomorrow.

"Listen cousin, I know you like Céline and I'm sorry to ask because you guys are tight," starts Billy. "But do you think she could have something to do with all of this mess?" he dares to ask.

"Céline?" I reply, staring at Billy, looking quite perplexed. "Hum. Never crossed my mind to be honest."

Billy hesitates to push forward.

"She's always been the smart one, you know. Plus, her and Marcus had kind of a *thing*, no? Always running off together for interviews and all. That shit sticks on you, no?" continues Billy, but this time offering up only pure speculations.

"Nah, forget about it. Céline and Marcus were just going through the motions and the schedule and all. We all did. Marcus has always been rather cold in that matter. He never dared to embarrass himself with relationships that were... too serious," I explain.

"You know, Marcus has many houses but no home."

A moment of silence.

"Well, we miss *you* partner!" jokes Billy while looking over-board into the dark waters below. "Hey, you down *there* champion? Come out for a drink, would you?"

"Hey stop it Billy, this is getting gloomy, okay?" I tell him. "I just need to wrap my mind around that ray gun thing. What a shit show. Using military-grade equipment just to prove a point? Just to win stupid wager?"

Sometimes it's hard to tell who's a villain and who's not. When we all dance in the dark, every heart is black.

The skipper who's been eavesdropping for the last ten minutes comes to meet us on the front banquette with a bottle of rum he had stashed in the console. That kid deserves a promotion.

As we pass the bottle around, the short fuse of Billy's constantly scheming mind lights up. He's getting agitated. "I got to admit cousin, I kinda like those odds Jackie mentioned this afternoon."

"You mean, the 20 to 1 odds *against me?*" I ask. "You like that, don't you? You little weasel!"

"Well, it's not really against you, Nolan. People just think something, somehow, will happen again during the event. Something that would prevent you from finishing the race. And you know what? I bet most of these people are in on it."

"You're right. Most of these wagers probably came from Angelo's cronies. People he owes money to or whatnot. People that he keeps in the loop for an easy payout."

"Exactly," says Billy with a finger in the air.

The skipper is quiet and listening, simply content to be sitting at the adults table for once.

"What if we could be certain to prevent another incident?" brainstorms Billy all of a sudden. "What if there was a way to prevent your car from shutting down all together?"

"Go on," I tell my cousin.

"In this case and according to this particular prompt bet, you wouldn't even need to *win* the race tomorrow, in order to beat the odds. All you would need to accomplish is to *finish* the goddamn race to collect that wager."

If Billy has even just one smart idea per year, that was it.

"You mean that you would bet on me? You would bet against

those 20 to 1 odds?" I ask Billy, my attention now caught in this sudden reversal of power and knowledge.

"Yeah, if we can stop their evil plan in their tracks, I think we could teach them a lesson," says Billy. "And we could take all of their fucking money."

"There must be a way. I just need a little more time," I mumble.

We all lean back in the leather seats to reflect, hoping that the circling bottle will bring a fresh perspective on the matter at hand. We lost all the cocaine we had when we jumped ship and abandoned our clothes aboard the yacht.

I'd pay a million bucks for a sports bag right now.

"Hey Skippy," snaps Billy to our young captain, reading my mind. "Got *anything* on you by any chance? You know, a small picture of the holy spirit inside the pocket of that jacket?"

So many ways to ask drugs to a stranger.

"Any way we can secure a direct line to the Columbia's embassy?"

He's good.

But the skipper quickly has enough of the riddles and cuts to the chase.

"If you want, I can take you to *The Pirate Cove* right now," the skipper tells us. "It's where all of the crew members of those charter yachts will go to hang out tonight after work. I'm pretty sure we can find almost anything out there."

By the holy fucking spirit.

There is a place the rich kids call *The Pirate Cove.*

"I was planning to go anyway, once I'd be done with you guys," explains the skipper.

"Well, you're definitely not done with us, my friend," says Billy, standing up and chugging the last gulp of rum. He then throws the bottle into the sea.

We get the message.

"Let's fucking go."

Maybe there is a small chance our poor souls might be rescued tonight after all.

30

The Pirate Cove

The Pirate Cove is not just a place, but also *a moment.*

Every month on the night of the full moon, local rich kids and crew members from the superyachts will gather in this secret bay about a mile east of the walls of the Fortress.

Once there, they will begin to tie together using ropes, an ensemble of barges, dinghy and small boats that will ultimately form a giant floating island just for the night.

As we approach with the speedboat, we begin to see the warm glow of torches slowly detouring the edges of a distant party. The rhythms and the music can't reach us yet, but somehow, I can feel the attraction in my chest.

A magical place, but also *a moment* in time where you had to be there.

Ephemeral.

Billy and I stand at the bow. My cousin puts his foot on the ledge to sport the captain's pose, instructing the young skipper to blow full steam ahead. This is fucking exciting.

The three of us are now totally obsessed and attracted to the elements that begin to unfold on the horizon as we're cutting the distance.

There must be something like 30 boats and rafts already tied up around a central barge, where the bulk of the kids are dancing. Some are beating drums at the foot of a massive DJ booth carved out of a solid block of ice.

A kid with a flare gun is firing red bulbs in the air and motions where we should bring the speedboat around. No one seems to be in distress here, except for us. We circle the giant barge to find a spot next to a gondola. We connect to become one with this floating organism. One with the mirage.

We then begin to make our way towards the central barge, jumping and carefully stepping from boat to boat.

We became one
with the mirage.
Securing our place
on the moodboard.

On the deck of the pontoon to my left, there is an open kitchen with a pizza oven spitting calzones to the hungry kids extending their arms from a jetski. Next to the pontoon, there's a dingy serving pink mojitos in red party cups, scooping the elixir straight from giant coolers. I don't see any money being exchanged. This has nothing to do with the 28 Euros gin & tonics they sell to the tourists back at The Fortress.

Fireworks in the sky above us.

On a giant inflatable banana, a row of boys and girls are performing a massage chain while passing down a joint that came up stream, from a canoe drifting by.

Some of these kids are wearing wooden island masks. Others have ornamented their skin with blue and purple fish scales, marking their skin with glowing paint.

And they're all vibing in harmony to the beat of the drums that intensifies as we get closer to the central barge. Someone hands me a wooden mask that I immediately put on to get into the spirit. We see more boats and kids joining the party. The island is growing.

No one here seems to care *who* we are or *what* we do. They all answer to nicknames only.

All the party without the race.
Full access without the face.
Totally free, at last.

On the edges of this floating island, more boys and girls swim or simply float on paddle boards, flamingo floaties and inflatable treasure chests. Fluorescent lights have been installed below the water, which diffuse a soft glow underneath their feet.

We haven't secured any drugs yet, but it feels like I'm already high on something. Drifting away with a bunch of lost boys and girls. All living for the night. All safe from the conflicts of The Fortress.

"We got here just in time for the moon ritual!" shouts the skipper. "They're gonna bring the DJ at 10:10 sharp. It's a thing they do every time."

More fireworks.

"Did you forget your mission?" asks Billy to the skipper, the drugs always on his mind. Especially now that our brains have exploded due to the overpowered stimulation of everything and everyone around.

"Follow me," says the skipper. "The King Crab has what we need!" he tells Billy, while pointing at some rusty fishing vessel a couple of ropes away in front of us.

"You guys take care of the loot, I'll grab some beers over here while I wait for you," I tell them.

My cousin and the skipper tip toe away towards the metal vessel while I find myself a seat at some makeshift bar on the edge of the catamaran. My feet dangle in the water. I start to feel a little concerned at the obscurity below.

"Aren't you worried we might all turn into a shark buffet?" I ask the girl behind the bar.

"Unless they enjoy the EDM pumping, I don't think there's a living fish a mile around with that bass," she explains. "What do you want to drink?"

"Hum, can I get three beers?"

"You're cute," she says, handing me a large plastic bucket filled with a mixture I believe to be rum & cola. She then throws three bamboo straws in the mix. "There you go, *papi*."

I take a sip. Yes, it's rum and coke.

Suddenly, a woman wearing a mermaid tail emerges from the water and perches right next to me at the bar. She looks at me straight in the eyes while leaning forward to take a giant sip from the bucket I'm still holding like an idiot.

"Are you... a real mermaid?" I ask, starstruck.

"Maybe."

She then kisses me on the cheek. "Catch me if you can!" she shouts before diving back in the deep blue.

Someone detonates more fireworks in the distance and all the kids start cheering underneath subsequent flashes of green, blue, and yellow. The additional glare allows me to detach the shapes of Billy and the skipper awkwardly dodging sailboat masts and clinging to various ropes as they make their way back from the King Crab vessel.

"Look at what we found!" says Billy with his hand open, presenting me with a bunch of white pills. Just a happy dog who found a stick.

"Oh boy, what is it?" I ask, a little hesitant.

"It's *Ritalin,*" says the skipper. "You can buy this stuff with no script almost anywhere on the coast."

"It will bring us back on the level," says Billy. "Until we can find some more fish scales, you know."

I look at the white pills again.

"The King Crab captain said one pill should be enough," explains Billy before putting two inside his mouth. We do the same while the barmaid transfers more alcohol into the bucket with a plastic hose. Shoutout to Archimedes.

More mermaids begin to circle the bar, so it's time for us to move.

31

The Moon Ritual

"I believe it's kicking in!" shouts Billy, holding on to the mast of a rolled-up sail to avoid falling between the hulls of the boats.

"Oh you believe so?" I shout back, looking at the young skipper balancing the rum & cola bucket on his head.

"I'm way more focused now, look," the kid is telling us.

The effects of ingesting *Ritalin* (when you don't need it) is quite a challenge to describe beyond the medical terms. For now, it feels like my body is totally drunk, but my head is super sharp.

It's like I'm receiving the data and processing it just fine. But then, there is a slight delay in the chain of command my brain is talking to the rest of my limbs. Provoking a flunky puppet-like parade as the three of are trying to make it to the center barge in time before they start *The Moon Ritual*.

Yet again, in my mind, sharp as fuck.

I mean I can see distances super clearly, and you could ask me anything and I believe I could pull some insights from some of my past lives spent on this planet.

"Here we go!" says the skipper.

"In case this pirate adventure goes south, remind me who's your emergency contact?" I ask my cousin.

"Last time I checked, that was you!" says Billy.

"Oh boy."

"Hey, maybe drop a pin to Céline or something? Just in case," he adds.

I'm looking at the G–Shock and it's 10:10 pm.

Suddenly the music completely stops, and all the kids begin to howl at the full moon.

It's fantastic.

Billy and the skipper laugh, and both start howling at the moon too. I'm just trying to take it all in. Never to forget this moment we almost missed.

That everyone else on this planet seems to be missing.

"Man, I don't wanna go back," I tell Billy.

"Happy Birthday cousin!" he shouts, fist in the air.

"Hold on, it's your birthday Nolan?" asks the skipper.

"No. It's not. Long story," I tell him.

"When is your birthday, then?" he inquires.

"May six," I tell him. "I'm a Taurus."

"Wait, what did you say?" asks Billy.

"I'm a fucking Taurus baby!"

"No before that? Your exact date of birth?" he keeps asking.

"May six. Five-o-six. Why?" I ask, confused.

"506 Nolan!" screams Billy caught up in some sort of an epiphany. "506! That's the number of the room that goes with the key card," he explains, now putting it all together.

"How could we have missed that?" I tell him. "Damn, we have to go back now. We have to go back and check out the room before the end of the night. This booking might expire tomorrow at some point!"

Meanwhile on the central barge, a set of two characters are taking their place. A man and woman, both wearing wooden

---

Dangling in the Air

...uck or grand design, room 506 was situated right ...outdoor terrace of Mickey's penthouse and his never-...rty. Therefore, a twenty-foot drop would indeed get ...o the other balcony below. Unfortunately, without ...o break our fall, we're looking at a broken neck or ...least. Which in my particular case, is simply not in ...Because I'd like to remind everyone that I have an ...race tomorrow.

...Mickey's penthouse, a whole new crowd has now ...the private quarters since our last dip earlier this ...One night closer to the championship, and I have a ...we've moved to an upper and more succulent tier ...ls' segmentation.

...midnight, I always like to hit the refresh button," ...Mickey. And that, without adding any more expla-...t when the guy might potentially sleep or at least ...a home cooked meal. He must have been training masks and red cloaks over their shoulders. They are slowly making their way towards the ice block of the DJ booth.

Rows of kids separate and bow down as the characters take their place at the front. Some are throwing confetti and rice above the crowd. This must be the moon ritual.

The couple in the red capes then turn around and lift their arms together in the air.

That's when I see it.

Oh, I could recognize that black swimsuit anywhere in the world.

She's here. Natalia.

All of a sudden and perfectly on cue, the music and the bass drop and all the kids start jumping in the air. The barge gets so agitated, it's getting hard to stand up. The Moon Ritual is complete, and this party is now a total *rager*.

"Natalia!" I try to scream but it's pointless. The music is too loud.

I know it's her. I know it's her behind that mask.

Trying to rush across the dance floor, we push and toss people aside as we try to get closer to the small stage where the characters are still worshiping the sky and the full moon.

"Natalia!" I scream again. This t
in my direction.

And for a quick instant, I can se

Immediately she starts to race r
I try to rush towards her posit
follow the red cape gliding from
Just like a thief in the night.

Where are you going, sorceres

"Natalia, wait!" I push again.

It's too late though. She jur
it loose. I turn to Billy and th
behind me.

"Guys, get the boat, fast!" I

When I turn back towards N
in the distance, lights fadi
along with her blond hair i

The same image she gave r
cliff.

Natalia.

My lovely spy.

for this marathon for a while now. Or maybe it's just pills. Probably the pills.

One of the models brushes past my arm. She sports that alien from Venus aesthetic, with zero breast and minimal makeup. One slick back ponytail and clear eyes that blink just once a minute.

Another one of these apparitions is drinking from a coffee mug that says CHAMPAGNE. Warm vapors of cherry wood floating in her wake. Artificial yet on point.

Mickey, in the bedroom, is busy taking snapshots of another group of space invaders wearing all metallic bodysuits and pointing blow dryers in the air to act as fusion rifles.

"Say cheese!" he shouts in his signature tagline.

"You really wanna crawl down to 506?" asks Billy.

We both look around the room for a dangerous plan.

"Maybe call Céline first? Again, just to let her know where we are? Insurance stuff. I mean, in case she must send the *medivac* to rappel us out of trouble."

"Rappel down, that's a good plan!" I tell my cousin.

While Billy wrestles the space invaders on the bed in order to harvest the sheets from underneath them, I attempt a quick call to Céline.

We both look
around the room
for a dangerous
plan.

"She's not picking up, that never happens," I shout.

"Maybe she's meditating?" he says.

"*Meditating?*" I ask him. "It's past midnight. What is she trying to do? Sync up with the whales' songs or something?"

I send her a text message: *DANGLING IN THE AIR. CALL ME BACK.*

My cousin and Mickey are now assembling all those sheets into a continuous lifeline, hoping it's gonna support our full weight while we transition from balcony to balcony.

"You think it's gonna hold up?" asks Billy.

"These are Egyptian quality bed sheets with a 1500 thread count, boys. Only luxury for Mickey," our host mentions, speaking of himself in the third person. Something he does quite a lot actually.

I like Mickey. He keeps on dancing while the world outside is burning.

"Man, I don't wanna go back," I tell Billy.

"Happy Birthday cousin!" he shouts, fist in the air.

"Hold on, it's your birthday Nolan?" asks the skipper.

"No. It's not. Long story," I tell him.

"When is your birthday, then?" he inquires.

"May six," I tell him. "I'm a Taurus."

"Wait, what did you say?" asks Billy.

"I'm a fucking Taurus baby!"

"No before that? Your exact date of birth?" he keeps asking.

"May six. Five-o-six. Why?" I ask, confused.

"506 Nolan!" screams Billy caught up in some sort of an epiphany. "506! That's the number of the room that goes with the key card," he explains, now putting it all together.

"How could we have missed that?" I tell him. "Damn, we have to go back now. We have to go back and check out the room before the end of the night. This booking might expire tomorrow at some point!"

Meanwhile on the central barge, a set of two characters are taking their place. A man and woman, both wearing wooden masks and red cloaks over their shoulders. They are slowly making their way towards the ice block of the DJ booth.

Rows of kids separate and bow down as the characters take their place at the front. Some are throwing confetti and rice above the crowd. This must be the moon ritual.

The couple in the red capes then turn around and lift their arms together in the air.

That's when I see it.

Oh, I could recognize that black swimsuit anywhere in the world.

She's here. Natalia.

All of a sudden and perfectly on cue, the music and the bass drop and all the kids start jumping in the air. The barge gets so agitated, it's getting hard to stand up. The Moon Ritual is complete, and this party is now a total *rager*.

"Natalia!" I try to scream but it's pointless. The music is too loud.

I know it's her. I know it's her behind that mask.

Trying to rush across the dance floor, we push and toss people aside as we try to get closer to the small stage where the characters are still worshiping the sky and the full moon.

"Natalia!" I scream again. This time, the wooden mask dents in my direction.

And for a quick instant, I can see her, and she can see me.

Immediately she starts to race right behind the DJ booth, while I try to rush towards her position. Behind the ice cube, I can follow the red cape gliding from gondola to gondola, so elegant. Just like a thief in the night.

Where are you going, sorceress? Beautiful merchant of doubt.

"Natalia, wait!" I push again. "I just want to know *why?*"

It's too late though. She jumps on a jet ski and starts to cut it loose. I turn to Billy and the skipper who were tagging just behind me.

"Guys, get the boat, fast!" I order.

When I turn back towards Natalia, the jet ski is already gliding in the distance, lights fading. The magical red cloak dancing along with her blond hair in the back.

The same image she gave me that day we drove together by the cliff.

Natalia.

My lovely spy.

32

Dangling in the Air

By pure luck or grand design, room 506 was situated right below the outdoor terrace of Mickey's penthouse and his never-ending party. Therefore, a twenty-foot drop would indeed get us down to the other balcony below. Unfortunately, without anything to break our fall, we're looking at a broken neck or an ankle at least. Which in my particular case, is simply not in the cards. Because I'd like to remind everyone that I have an important race tomorrow.

Inside of Mickey's penthouse, a whole new crowd has now populated the private quarters since our last dip earlier this afternoon. One night closer to the championship, and I have a feeling that we've moved to an upper and more succulent tier of the models' segmentation.

"At around midnight, I always like to hit the refresh button," confessed Mickey. And that, without adding any more explanation about *when* the guy might potentially sleep or at least sit down for a home cooked meal. He must have been training for this marathon for a while now. Or maybe it's just pills. Probably the pills.

One of the models brushes past my arm. She sports that alien from Venus aesthetic, with zero breast and minimal makeup. One slick back ponytail and clear eyes that blink just once a minute.

Another one of these apparitions is drinking from a coffee mug that says CHAMPAGNE. Warm vapors of cherry wood floating in her wake. Artificial yet on point.

Mickey, in the bedroom, is busy taking snapshots of another group of space invaders wearing all metallic bodysuits and pointing blow dryers in the air to act as fusion rifles.

"Say cheese!" he shouts in his signature tagline.

"You really wanna crawl down to 506?" asks Billy.

We both look around the room for a dangerous plan.

"Maybe call Céline first? Again, just to let her know where we are? Insurance stuff. I mean, in case she must send the *medivac* to rappel us out of trouble."

"Rappel down, that's a good plan!" I tell my cousin.

While Billy wrestles the space invaders on the bed in order to harvest the sheets from underneath them, I attempt a quick call to Céline.

We both look
around the room
for a dangerous
plan.

"She's not picking up, that never happens," I shout.

"Maybe she's meditating?" he says.

"*Meditating*?" I ask him. "It's past midnight. What is she trying to do? Sync up with the whales' songs or something?"

I send her a text message: *DANGLING IN THE AIR. CALL ME BACK.*

My cousin and Mickey are now assembling all those sheets into a continuous lifeline, hoping it's gonna support our full weight while we transition from balcony to balcony.

"You think it's gonna hold up?" asks Billy.

"These are Egyptian quality bed sheets with a 1500 thread count, boys. Only luxury for Mickey," our host mentions, speaking of himself in the third person. Something he does quite a lot actually.

I like Mickey. He keeps on dancing while the world outside is burning.

You see, it's not much the individual sheets that I'm worried about, but rather the connection between them. Céline hasn't called me back yet. We'll have to venture into the void on our own and without her holding my hand this time.

Now who's gonna secure the other end of the chain? Most of these girls are less than a hundred pounds.

"Ladies and... ladies!" Starts Mickey, motioning to the young models to gather around in the living room. "We're gonna play a little game and escort these gentlemen down to safety. Yes, yes, yes unfortunately they must abandon the comfort of our little piece of heaven up here, for the treacherous hell of the mortals below."

They seem to get it.

"Hop hop now, my angels!" Mickey says.

Billy goes first over the ledge while the girls, Mickey and I clench to the bed sheets in a tense tug-o-war formation. Slowly and cautiously, we lower my cousin until he finally gets a foot on the marble balcony of room 506 below.

Then, it's my turn to go downstream on Jacob's ladder.

One last look at the floor above. Mickey Mouse and his court are jubilating. Some might save a country, others just a puppy. The feeling of contribution in this world is always relative. The point is, tonight this ensemble of creatures of the night successfully escorted us further down our quest line. Helping us gather yet another piece of the puzzle.

We step inside. Room 506 is kind of small and immaculate.

We turn on all the lights.

The bed is still tucked, the ice bucket untouched and the TV remote is standing on guard on top of the television.

The safe is open. Nothing inside.

"You think it's the right room?" asks Billy.

Suddenly a hint. On the nightstand, my cousin picks up an eyeball glass with some red lipstick on it.

"Sorceress," I mutter.

The rest of the room is untouched, almost puzzling.

It's only when I turn around towards the exit that I finally see it.

The painting hangs on the wall of the hotel room.

The girl holding the scorpion.

"Pick it up!" says Billy with such excitement. "Look behind it, there might be something. A clue or a message or something."

I pick up the painting and flip it around. Nothing.

"Hum."

"Maybe it's another one of those riddles?" asks my cousin. "What is the painting about?" he asks.

"It's about a girl holding both the venom and the antidote. Friend and foe. Pleasure and pain," I explain, giving him the cliff notes. "At least that's what I get from it."

"Fucking riddles," mumbles Billy, popping another Ritalin from the stash. Hopefully, it will take effect soon enough to decipher this next clue.

"Well, it's safe to say that we already know what the venom is, right? That thing in the video. That ray gun. That's what paralyzed you on the racetrack, right?"

"Yes. And then?"

Billy is clearly on to something.

"What *exactly* did happen the moment you were *stung?*" he asks, recounting the chain of unfortunate events during qualifications.

"Then all the lights went off," I simply reply.

Holy shit.

"That's it!" he screams. "That's it! Turn off all the lights."

We quickly bounce around the room like two madmen trying to extinguish every source of light.

And there it is.

Behind the painting, someone had written a message using glow in the dark finger paint. Someone had written the name: FARADAY.

It's time to wake up the Captain. He will know what this means.

Michael Faraday was an English scientist who contributed to the study of electromagnetism and electrochemistry. In 1821, he invented the electric motor, and in 1831 he made the first dynamo, known as the Faraday disc, a forerunner of today's electrical generator.

TLDR: he was a major nerd.

It is even said that Albert Einstein himself kept a picture of Faraday on his study wall throughout the years and credited Faraday for being one of the greatest scientific discoverers of all time.

Faraday also gave his name to a peculiar invention called the Faraday Cage. He made the first prototype in 1836 which consists of a large box lined up with wire mesh. To test his invention, Faraday zapped it from the outside with electricity while he stood safely inside. The device had the power to protect from electromagnetic charges.

The phone rings five times.

"Nolan, what the hell? It's almost 2 am," scuffs The Captain on the phone.

"Captain, we got it!" I rush to say. "We know how to counteract the ray gun!"

"Go on," he replies, now sounding 50% less pissed.

"It has something to do with the Faraday principles…" I explain.

"Oh wow boys, so you think you're smart now? We thought about this already! We cannot build a cage around your car. This is ludicrous. What drugs are you on? And is that little weasel cousin of yours with you again?"

"I know Captain, I know. But hear me out. What if you could run some kind of electric current on the fuselage. Maybe we could turn the car into a giant magnet?"

A long pause.

"A force field. Interesting," we just hear the Captain say on the other end of the line.

"Could this be something?" I ask. "Captain?"

"I'm still here," he says.

Another pause.

"Okay, let me sound the alarm and gather all the engineers we got into the hangar. We'll try to come up with something before the sun rises."

The Captain clicks off.

Billy stares at me with dollar signs in his eyes.

We just went from zero to a hundred real quick.

33

The Exotic Gardens

"Some of these plants are more than a hundred years old," reads Céline from the plaque above a cluster of shiny plants named *succulents*.

"So what? They never go anywhere," I reply.

Billy is here too, pointing the silver gun he stole yesterday in Angelo's office towards the bronze statue of Prince Albert, feigning a standoff.

"Did you sleep with that gun?" shouts Céline.

"He's on the phone," I tell her.

"And why is he so fucking jolly all the time?" she asks.

"Every morning I crush a chocolate cookie into his cereal," I kinda joke.

It's a glorious Sunday morning here in the suspended and exotic St Martin Gardens. The view over the Portier's Cove and the infinite blue sea beyond is simply gorgeous.

"Should we go check the underground cave next?" asks Céline, eyes still on the brochure.

"I'm good. We had our fair share of the underworld yesterday, I tell you."

She's up to speed. I told her everything. The pirate cove, the ritual, the hotel room riddle. Apparently, the Captain and his engineers came up with a sound plan that they are excited to unveil.

I'm really glad we all went to bed last night after that phone call. Now I feel fresh and confident to tackle the race this afternoon. Most drugs flushed out of my system already.

Céline is looking pretty amid the wild flowers. She had time to freshen up, plus she wears that perfume that I like.

"That smell," I tell her. "That's the only constant as we move from city to city."

She blushes. But now is not the time to reopen an old case.

Cousin Billy is on the phone with Mr. Stanley, the family accountant. He's very good. Today for lunch, he's gonna lick sixty envelopes.

Somewhere during the summer of junior high, Billy's mom bought him a pager, so she could kinda know where he was and check on us once in a while. Next thing you know, Billy was selling drugs to guys twice his age, using the pager number as a dispatch.

That particular summer, we both understood the necessity to tell a good story. And always have something to sell.

Billy moves his hands a lot as he's talking to someone across the ocean. "Yeah Stanley, listen. Nolan and I need to withdraw five million *each* before noon. All cash of course," he explains to the accountant on the phone.

After our conversation with the Captain last night, and after he promised to pull an all-nighter to find a solution to the Faraday challenge, Billy and I felt confident that these geniuses would ultimately come up with an *antidote* to our magnetic bazooka problem.

That's when we agreed to take on a little wager of our own, based on those fantastic odds detailed earlier by Casino Jackie. If we could manage to counter spell the ray gun in time, and successfully get my car over that finish line in one piece, there was a good chance we could stunt on these haters. Take all of their fucking money.

Odds paying 20 to 1.

And you know what? It is worth a shot just to see Angelo's face when it happens.

Another spaghettini trying to punch above its weight class.

Billy still quacks over the railing. "That's right, five million from my account, and another crispy five large croissants from Nolan's account. Transferred ASAP to the Bank of Monaco," Billy instructs our treasurer.

You could say that this is a rich people problem.

Another spaghettini
trying to punch
above its weight
class.

"No Stanley, we're not held hostage or anything. Jesus. It's for *personal use*," my cousin reassures the accountant. Then he turns to me. "Nolan, just say hi to Stanley, would you?" He hands me the phone.

"Hi Stanley. Yeah, we're fine, thank you. Did you get my Christmas card?" I ask the poor man we probably just pulled out of bed, due to the time zone difference. "What Christmas card? Well, all of them!" I tell the accountant.

"He's Jewish, you idiot," says Billy, plucking the phone back from my hand.

Céline joins us on the garden terrace where in the glittering distance, we can admire the super yachts coming in and out of the blue bay. Most of these giant toys retailing in the hundreds of millions a pop. Everything so relative. Measuring cocks in yards now.

The garden sprawls over a good part of the cliff. Certainly, the priciest *luzerne* per square foot in Europe.

"Love you, Stanley, kiss your wife for me, would you?" Billy hangs up. Then walks confidently towards us, the silver gun tucked in along with his Armani silk shirt. Despicable.

"So what's the plan, cousin? Stanley still trusts you, I see?" I ask Billy.

"Funny guy. The ten million will be transferred to the Bank of Monaco as of right now. Stanley says he knows a guy that will expedite the whole thing. There, we can fill up the duffle bags and covertly make our way into the Casino. Just in time to place that wager with Jackie. Before the betting window closes," he explains.

"Just like that?" asks Céline.

"Just like that," says Billy. "You gotta love the kingdom."

Céline looks in the distance for a moment. "Boys, what about me?" she finally asks. "How can I get *in* on that action?"

"We'll split the pot three ways if we win," I assure her.

Billy lifts his chin, he agrees.

Céline totally deserves it. All these years, she was squeezed between us and management. That payout could be her golden ticket to whatever she used to dream about when she was just a girl.

Oh, Marcus would have loved this clever plan. Trust me. The fact that we stick it to them. The fact that we refuse to back away and double down at the very last moment.

He would have been really proud, at last.

34

Out of the Bank Vault

You might think that ten million in cash is a lot to carry around, but you can actually shove it all inside three *Louie* bags.

The money has been prepared as promised. Stacks of crispy US 100$ bills. They're used to it, I suppose.

You might think
that ten million in
cash is a lot to carry
around, but you can
actually shove it all
inside three *Louie*
bags.

The city state of Monaco is home to more millionaires per capita than anywhere else in the world. There are literally zero homeless people. If you spot one, it's called fashion.

Many decide to move here every year, bringing along fortunes and a lot of secrets into this tax-free enclave nestled on the French Riviera. All very confidential. Making it also one of the most expensive parcels of real estate on the planet. A chunk of land they keep expanding into the sea with ambitious new developments and projects such as The Emerald Tower.

Who said we can't print new land?

There is so much money on this small rock that our cash withdrawal this morning won't raise any eyebrows.

Somewhere under the bedrock, inside of the private vault of The Bank of Monaco, a banker has to recount the money in front of us with these swift machines that go super fast. Spitting equal and very satisfying stacks just like in the movies.

Stack it up, tie it up, put it in the bag.
Stack it up, tie it up, put it in the bag.

The bank and the underground vault are glorious feats of architecture. Roman arches, checkered floors and Victorian chandeliers. No doubt, the Freemasons built this place.

I don't really know what to think about banks, honestly.
Except that it's better to be on their good side.

A knife can do good, and a knife can do bad.

Once we're all set and the money count is right, we zip up the duffle bags to the gills, sign up the paperwork, and the banker gently escorts us towards the exit. It's out of their hands now.

"Do you want me to call the valet?" asks the banker.

"We're good. We're parked just up the curb," says Billy. He means that we left the green convertible with the blinkers flashing right there on the sidewalk. What's a potential parking ticket if not another chance to gamble in this town?
But once we clear the bank doors, the elevator music halts with a scratch the moment we spot three of Angelo's gorillas waiting by the car. Someone inside the bank must have tipped them off. It's a small fucking town.
We see them, they see us. There might be three hundred yards at most between our position and the heavies. Something they could swing pretty easy.

"What do we do *now*?" asks Billy, holding dear to his duffle bag. I guess he realizes we're not kids anymore. And that these guys no longer play poker with crackers.

Two options. We can either go in the direction of the car, which is fucking stupid. Or we can shoot straight for the casino. In that case, we'll have to clear maybe a thousand yards in order to make it safely to the front door.

"It's a no brainer," says Billy.

"You're a no brainer," says Céline.

"Forget the car, run!" I shout, taking the lead towards the Casino. Billy and Céline have zero choice but to follow.

Immediately the gorillas launch into a hot pursuit. One of these days, the dog will get the mailman. But not today. Oh not today.

I've never been more excited to run with bags full of money.

"What are you doing, stupid?" asks Céline, sprinting the best she can next to me. Both clenching to a giant bag the weight of a small child. "They're gonna get us once we reach the casino anyways," she exhales.

"They can't get in," shouts Billy from behind.

"What?" says Céline.

Billy is right. Locals are not allowed inside the Monte Carlo Casino. We know it, they know it. That's why they speed it up a notch.

Princess Caroline is the one credited with establishing gambling casinos in Monaco to support the House of Grimaldi, the ruling family of Monaco at the time in order to save them from bankruptcy. Also insisting that they could only plunder the money from outsiders, never their own.

Running down the alley, Billy topples a fruit cart. He quickly reaches into the duffle bag for a fresh stack of 100$ and simply throws it at the problem. This seems to be a recurring pattern for him.

Bad guys are closing in.

Instead of looping around the fountain, we splash right through it, with water almost to our knees and the duffle bags over our heads. This is now a special op, and we're on the extraction team.

The first doorman who sees us approaching at full pace recognizes Billy and me from yesterday. He quickly clears open the Casino doors, and the three of us slide smoothly into the controlled climate of the biosphere.

Safe. With the apes stuck outside.

Security hands us cushy hotel bathrobes before we finally walk in. Like three housewives heading down for a mud rub at the spa. Leaving all problems at the door.

The three gorillas are immediately confronted by security who rejects their local passports. Their desperate roars and slurs are slowly fading away in the distant canopy. We already took care of texting Jackie. Telling her to expect us in the betting lounge with three suitcases full of fireworks.

"My minions!" boasts Casino Jackie the moment we roll in with a brass hotel chariot on which we've stack the duffle bags full of cash.

"Still time for an extra wager, Jackie?" I ask, kicking the luggage cart in her direction.

"Of course. The books will close in an hour. What do you got for Jackie?" she asks, rubbing her manta hands together.

"We would like to lay these ten million on a prompt bet," explains Billy. "We want to bet these ten million that my man, Nolan here, will finish the race."

"What are the odds for that *now*?" asks Céline.

Jackie pulls out the notebook.

"Adding those ten larges to the book will flatten the odds *10 to 1*, on that particular wager," the human computer spits out.

"Lock it in," I tell Jackie. "And you keep the bags. Would you?"

We just took a giant leap of faith. Now let's hope science is on our side. Let's hope the Captain and his team deliver on the solution.

The money is safe here with Jackie and backed up by the Casino. I gave the wager ticket to Céline. She stares at it for a moment.

"That was smooth," she says, holding a ticket the size of a pizza voucher that is now worth the equivalent of a small plane.

Now let's go find out what the Captain has come up with.

35

Surrounded by Crows

Management has just landed from their cloud in order to fix whatever they think is broken. And here I am, about to be backed up in a corner. About to be asked to answer questions regarding some specifics when in reality, even what happened last night is still kinda blurry in my mind.

These types of meetings usually take place in comfy private airport lounges where we only speak to management through the small box of a speaker phone. A position of power in which Céline takes the lead while I reserve myself the option to put the speaker on mute for a couple of seconds, whenever I need to retreat and regroup.

Or at worst, I might have to rub shoulders with these international money hoarders plus their wives maybe once a year, during the annual investors banquet. With formalities and a million people between us.

But today, no cheese plates and cold cuts. Management called a sit down.

We hence find ourselves squeezed in a cold conference room at some hotel. Could be a morgue. It was sunny outside, but now it's overcast. They smelled blood. Fucking vultures.

You could say I've never been good with figures of authority. In fact, I like to steal a pencil every time I go to the office. And so far, I have two pencils.

The president of the board is already perched at the opposite end of the long conference table, so I quietly take my seat next to Céline, trying my best not to look the sun directly in the eyes.

"Nolan, are you okay?" starts the President.

"I'm fine. Full night of sleep. Ready to go," I quickly feed to the flock of black crows gathered around the table. All wearing oversized suits and ties. The guy to my left is so bloated, they must have built the room around him.

"How do you explain what happened during qualifications?" the President inquires.

Hum, let's recap, *shall we?*

Some shady real estate developer tried to rig the race, collect a wager, and save his crumbling empire. The plan was apparently involving your golden boy Marcus, in cahoots with the girl that I liked a lot. Who now appears to be more of a role-playing sorceress. Unfortunately for them, their whole deal went south the moment Marcus disappeared. And now I guess their *plan B* is to shoot me down with a covert magnetic canon. Any questions?

Taking a brief look around the table, I quickly regain my composure before I ruffle any feathers.

"We're working on it," I just replied instead, deflecting responsibility by looking in the direction of the Captain.

"The malfunction has been addressed," concurs the chief engineer.

The president opens up a file that was laid in front of him. "We have officially begun our search for a replacement this morning," he swings back at me. Just like that. No gloves.

"Looking for *my new partner?*" I ask the President.

"We're looking for a whole new team, Nolan," he replies.

"*Excuse* me?" jumps Céline, totally blindsided.

"I'm sorry Nolan. Investors are very nervous right now. They believe it's simply best to refresh the whole roaster altogether. Bring a new champion on board, along with his *protégé* for the rest of the season," explains the chief vulture officer, talons on the table.

The balls on these birds. If they void my contract, what am I? Another rebel without a clause?

The goons had guns, but these guys have lawyers.

"This is ridiculous Mr. President," I allow myself to object right away. "It's been only 24 hours and we still don't even know yet what happened to Marcus! And yet, you guys are already talking about replacing *both of* us? Unbelievable."

Silence.

The goons had guns, but these guys have lawyers.

For a moment, the crows all turn to the President, then turn back to me in sync, then back to the President. As if a frontier town duel was about to go down on main street.

I shoot first.

"I got this, guys. We can win this race today. We can show them! I just need a little more time," I plead with the board of raptors.

"I'm afraid you don't have any more time, Nolan. Either you win the race this afternoon, or it's over, and we'll introduce the new team next weekend," the President finally rules out.

So this is it.

Placing the bet with Billy this morning had put me in a comfortable position, where I simply had to *finish* the race in order to secure the bag. But now, management made it clear that I also *need* to win in order to save my life.

And that is that.

36

Counter-Spell

We've all gathered in the hangar to hear about the Captain's plan to counter the ray gun that will be lurking in the tunnel. The race is two hours away, and the whole script just flipped into one of those heist movies. The Captain and a handful of engineers are standing next to a white board, on which they've drawn a map of the circuit. Scribbled next to it are physics formulas and assorted nerdy stuff.

The whole script
just flipped into one
of those heist
movies.

Two tough looking mechanics of our crew are guarding the door to the hangar. This shit is top secret. And we can't have the big birds from management pecking around.

"The solution we came up with, thanks to the insightful moonlight conversation I had with Nolan last night, is quite simple actually," says the Captain to kick off the presentation. I raise my coffee in acknowledgment.

"Our counterattack will be deployed in two parts. First, *the device.*"

The Captain flips the white board over to reveal a sketch of my race car. He also pulls out some kind of joystick, mounted with a red button. A makeshift device straight out of a Road Runner cartoon.

"As soon as we can confirm that the shooter is in place, Nolan, you will press that red button. At that moment, the battery pack that we've planted under the chassis will send a massive burst of energy through the coil circuit. They should create a force field around your car."

"Nice," whispers Céline.

"But here's the thing," the Captain goes on. "We can only pack enough juice inside of that battery to protect you for *one single lap.* Therefore, we're gonna have to activate the force field at the right moment. We only got one shot at deflecting that ray gun."

I raise my hand. "Hum, question. How will I know *when* to activate the force field?"

"That's the second part of the plan. *The scout.*"

We all look at each other.

"Of course, we can't send one of our guys out there. We need all hands-on deck. So, Billy, you will be the scout," instructs the Captain, pointing a finger at my cousin.

Billy straightens up on his chair, caught off guard by the teacher suddenly quizzing the classroom.

"Hum, scout, yeah sure. Roger that, Sir."

The Captain then moves on with the next crucial steps of the heist. He brings our attention towards the map of the circuit, on which an X marks the location where the shooter was spotted on the qualifications footage. A still frame of the shooter also has been pinned on the board. They really put the hours in.

"There is a service tunnel parallel to the racetrack. We believe that's how the shooter was able to sneak in and get right into position. Somewhere in that dark section over here," he points out on the map.

The Captain circles an area in the tunnel with a sharpie. Some service door.

"Your job, Billy, is to make your way up in the tunnel undetected, and update us through the radio. We need to know the exact moment the shooter is going to make his move."

"His or *her* move," I mumble.

"What was that?" asks the Captain.

"Nothing, go on," I shrug.

Billy raises his hand. "What if the bad guys try to reload for a *second shot?*" he asks, looking all smart.

"That's also on the table," replies the Captain. "At that point, we'll have to switch to analog."

"Meaning?" asks Billy, kinda perplexed.

"You'll have to go for the tackle, Billy. You will have to take down the shooter yourself. Any other questions?" the Captain wraps up.

Everyone gets up. We're ready to roll.

37

The Standoff

Angelo and I have reached the final table.

And there he is. Standing in our way as Céline, Billy and I are walking towards the launch pad. I wear my sunglasses in case this thing goes south.

It's the first time we meet again face to face, since that lame kidnapping attempt, or whatever you wanna call that. Catch and release, maybe. This time though, no proxy between us. Both of our entourages are holding back.

I wear my sunglasses
in case this thing
goes south.

It's a standoff. And the first one to speak will lose. So we just stare at each other.

It's too late to cause a scene anyways. Too late to alert the authorities that the race has been rigged. Too late to turn back since Billy and I put that ten million wager with Jackie. We can't screw this up. This is our scheme now.

It's Billy, Céline and I against the world.

It's funny. I remember one day back when I was just a kid playing on the street with Billy and my friends. We saw a small gleaming red car detour in the distance and coming in our direction. It was my dad, driving a used Miata he had just bought in some auction. It had cute lights and a dropped top. It was a beautiful summer day, and we had not a single care in the world.

And all my friends came out from everywhere. From the pools and the backyards and all just to take a look at that red car. I mean, it was just a Miata, but to us, it felt like a Ferrari. There might have been a dozen of us kids there on the street when my dad stopped by. We all jumped in. Some squeezing in the back and others sitting on the doors and the roll bar on top. And together with my dad, we slowly paraded the neighborhood. I mean, it was just a Miata.

But with your best friends, it turns to a Ferrari.

That's exactly how I feel right now. With Céline and Billy by my side and standing up to that prick.

"A change of heart?" asks Angelo finally, running a finger on his tacky pocket square. What a pompous look.

I don't say anything and just stare at him. My right hand hovering above my holster.

"We can still be friends, you know? We can still work this out," he continues, hinting at a potential last-minute deal. A *detente?*

With my left hand, I peel off my sunglasses. "It's too late for that. The books are closed," I tell him, before the three of us push through the blockade and towards the rocket. As I brush past his shoulder I whisper, "Don't blink."

Shit is about to hit the fan. And I'm the only one wearing a helmet.

I jump into the rocket, and the crew immediately begins to strap everything in place. It's showtime.

Céline comes by for a final check. "You're good?" she asks.

I raise a finger to my lips. "Shhhh. I got a thousand horses sleeping under that steel frame."

38

Waiting for That Green Light

If you could be anywhere in the world right now, where would it be? For me, it's right here. Waiting for that light to go green.

Despite my shortened performance during qualifications, I still managed to secure fifth place on the starting grid. Not far behind the Frenchmen and the Chinese dragons. I can see the open field ahead.

Time is about to slow down again, and all sounds will blend into a blur.

It's curious how far we've come over these last 48 hours.

Moments before Marcus disappeared on that yacht, he mentioned something that stuck with me ever since. He brushed off the fallen dust from the lapel of my tuxedo, then he looked straight into my eyes and asked, "Tell me Nolan. Underneath all that crap, is there someone that still wants to win?"

Now I kinda know what he meant.

Strapped inside that rocket with nowhere to go, except forward.

That's when the light turns green.

39

Debris

Lap 35.

I managed to climb to the fourth position, with the two Dragons and the Frenchmen, within my reach.

"Captain, I need new sneakers if I want to sprint past their position," I ask over the radio, signaling a pit stop.

"Come home, Nolan," the Captain replies.

As I make my move into the pit lane, Dragon junior does the same right in front of me. Perfect. I might be able to double him as we exit. It all depends on the pit stop execution now.

"Boys, let's make magic," I plead to the mechanics. "Touch and go. No time for soda."

A typical F1 pit stop can take less than three seconds, and in that time, the pit crew must accurately and efficiently change all four tires. Any mistakes or delays can cost a driver valuable positions on the track. The record time is 1.82 seconds. Though, I'm not asking for that much.

My car merges into position, and immediately, the four tire ballet begins to the sound of the compressed air drills. Two stations ahead in the pit lane, the Dragon is getting pampered as well.

One millennium, two millennium, three... And off he goes! Goddammit.

"Guys, let's wrap this up!" I scream, as my car finally drops to the ground. I smash the throttle. The Dragon beat me to it by merely two seconds, but I can still see him, as he launches back onto the racetrack at full speed. I follow.

Then there is a giant flash.

The Dragon was probably looking back at me as he exited the pits and didn't notice the tail end of the peloton cars swinging towards the exit ramp.

Two wheels stuck at the end of a toothpick. What could go wrong?

In an instant, his car and several others get obliterated. A group collision. At this speed, dreams don't just break. They shatter. Scratches, lights and sparkles. Followed by a wall of black fumes. I close my eyes and hope for a miracle. And to my surprise, I made it to the other side, unscathed.

At this speed,
dreams don't just
break.

They shatter.

The stewards will now wave the yellow flag for a couple of laps.

With the junior Dragon gone, I find myself in third position.

40

One Man Down

"It's fucking dark in here," describes Billy over the radio as he sneaks his way deeper into the maintenance tunnel.

"You're a good boy, Billy. Now go find that truffle," reminds the Captain.

It's lap 42.

They've cleaned up all the debris from the Dragon's crash and pilots are resuming maximum speed.

"This thing should happen at any moment now, no?" I ask through my helmet. "What's up on your end, Billy?"

I squeeze the makeshift red button between my legs, which we don't even know will work against the ray gun.

"I can't see anybody yet. What if they called it off?" asks Billy. "What if somebody told them we bet against them?"

"Keep going further down," instructs the Captain. "The shooter has to be there, somewhere."

"Maybe they changed the angle?" I ask, zooming by the packed stands in the harbor.

I'm about to enter the tunnel again, clenching my cheeks. Squinting my eyes. Another safe loop. But the sense of inevitability grows with every lap.

Every second, every minute, every year.

"I see something blinking down there," whispers Billy into his walkie-talkie. "Seems like that thing is still charging. And there's a dark shape crouched next to it. Someone is there with the device."

That sense of
inevitability grows
with every lap.

Every second,
every minute,
every year.

"Good, we got a visual," says the Captain, reassured.

Lap 44 now.

"The black jumpsuit is moving. I think it's happening guys!" says Billy.

"We need to be absolutely certain of that. We only got one shot in the tank!" warns the Captain. "That battery will create a force field for a minute, at most."

"Billy, I'm 20 seconds from entering the tunnel. What's the word?" I ask, negotiating the last curve.

"Shooter is moving into position. Oh shit. It's gonna be now, Nolan!" warns Billy over the radio.

"Press that button, Nolan!" instructs the Captain.

I close my eyes, and press the red button. With no idea if this device is even working.

The magnetic field of planet Earth is what protects us from the woes of the universe. It's what allows our species to stay into the race.

All of sudden, I see a blue glare flash on the nose of the fuselage.

"Shot fired!" confirms Billy into the radio.

"It's working! It's working!" I can't help but scream into the radio. "Something was deflected."

I smash down that throttle to flush out of the tunnel, hands in the air like a five year old busting out of a water slide.

"Oh captain, my captain!"

I can hear the whole engineering team clapping in the background.

"Back on track, Nolan. Now try to shave one more position. You still got one dragon left to chase, and he's right ahead of you."

"A dragon plus the Frenchman," I correct him.

"One at a time, Nolan. One at a time."

That Chinese kid is flying, I tell you that. When I'm this close to a passing, time slows down a bit more. It turns into a dogfight. You get confused about who is chasing who. You don't know what is up, or what is down. Only the checkered paint that garnishes the edge of the curves remind you of your position.

Not a moment to play fast and loose. More like tight and slow. Incisive. A meticulous dance of two pilots steering and hitting the brakes and steering back again.

Doors opening and closing.

Waiting for him to make that little mistake.

I'm chasing the Dragon in the long stretch of the circuit known as *the swimming pool.* He and I both know it won't happen here, not at this speed. Not on a straight line.

But right ahead comes the curb. An almost 90 degrees turn we're about to hit full clip. Wheel to wheel. And both of us are playing chicken as to who's gonna hit the brakes first.

Is it happening here? The moment he finally slips?

I'm pushing him into the trap.

That curb is closing in real fast, and I'm right there in his rear-view mirror, making sure he can read my sponsors.

One of his wheels hits the grass as he tries to shave a little too close. The tail spoiler of the dragon drifts a bit sideways, slowing him down. That's when I craft a slight and calculated turn on the inside, maneuvering out of the curb to sprint right ahead of the Chinese Dragon.

I'm in second place now.

More clapping in my helmet from the hangar team.

"Guys, I don't want to rain on the parade here," starts Billy, still crouched in the maintenance tunnel. "But it looks like the shooter is prepping for another shot."

"Damn, I'm almost there," I tell them. "Almost at the tunnel."

"Are you sure about that Billy? Can you confirm you have a

visual?" asks the Captain. "How far are you?"

"I'm three hundred yards away, maybe less. He hasn't seen me yet," confirms Billy.

He or she.

"Okay. The shooter is in position now! What do we do?" goes Billy, waiting for orders.

"I'm almost there!" I tell everyone.

"Plan B then. Go for the tackle, Billy!" orders the Captain over the radio.

We can hear my cousin's footsteps reverberating into the tunnel as he runs towards the shooter. He sounds out of breath.

"It's too far, I won't make it!" he tells us.

He has to. We got no more juice left in that battery.

"Run, Billy, run!" shouts the Captain.

"I'm not going down with the ship. Not this time," I tell them, clenching to the steering wheel as I enter the dark passage.

Loud footsteps in the tunnel. "Hey, you!" screams Billy.

That's when we hear a gunshot over the radio.

"I got him!" says Billy.

Oh shit, he still had that silver gun.

"Shot him in the back. He's down."

He or she.

But I can't worry about that right now. Gotta keep my eyes on the road and on the sandwiches.

We still hear Billy running down the tunnel, closing on the shooter.

I cross the starting line once again. Lap 47.

"There you are you fucking mole!" goes Billy, still on the radio. The ray gun didn't go off this time. That's one good thing.

"Take the helmet off Billy," I ask my cousin. "I need to know."

"You bet," Billy says.

Millions of seconds pass.

"Marcus? Oh fuck!" goes Billy, fighting the static over the radio.

"Marcus are you okay?"

41

Course Correction

The media was about to get what they wanted.

A picture of the champion, recovering in his bed at the villa.

Of course, they will never get the real story. Just the narrative. Nobody will know about the epic chase down the tunnel, nor the lone bullet fired from the silver gun that was lodged right between Marcus ribs. Which by some miracle, avoided any fatal damage.

A minor inconvenience, some would say.

Céline and Billy are making sure the bandages on Marcus's chest are well tucked and hidden under the bed sheets before the media harpies are let inside the room.

"Are we ready for the photo op?" asks Céline, hinting at the flock of photographers waiting on the other side.

"Actually, can you give us a moment?" I ask both of them, then wait for my cousin and Céline to leave.

"Do you need the gun?" jokes Billy on his way out.

I smile, then turn to my partner.

"Before we go on with the show, I gotta ask you *why*, Marcus? Why did you go through all of that trouble? And why did you leave me alone?" I ask him, now that he's no longer in a position to disappear on me.

Marcus looks through the window. The Mediterranean Sea glitters in the distance. Like fool's gold.

"You're just coasting, Nolan. Floating on the surface of things and people. Some shell of a man," he explains. "Something had to be done."

"Wait a minute. You went through all of this to *teach me a lesson?*" I ask.

You're just coasting.

Floating on the
surface of things
and people.

"Call it course correction, if you will," Marcus continues. "I had to Nolan. I needed to. The man I met years ago, the man who was stealing exotic cars to speed up on the rink with hopes of escaping a forsaken hometown. That man was no longer riding by my side."

It's my turn to gaze out the window. The tall pines are bending in the wind on each side of the balcony, trying to keep up.

"The drugs, the women, the money. Everything. That's just your new cruising speed. And sooner or later, you're gonna hit a wall."

I look at my feet for a moment. Ashamed to admit he's right.

"You found me once, Nolan. And I wanted you to find me again," Marcus says.

"That fire. It's still burning inside of me Marcus. We can still win together," I pledge to my master.

"I know that. Trust me, I know," he acknowledges. "You rose to the challenge, and I have to concede that I was quite impressed how you performed out there alone."

"Hell yeah," I tell him.

"All odds were stacked against you, but you guys managed to stick it to them," he continues. "You know, when Angelo came to me with that stupid proposal to rig the race, I figured it was my opportunity to teach you all a lesson."

I like Marcus. He reminds you of your rightful place in the world.

"You remember how much I can't stand cheaters, right?" he adds.

"Now I gotta tell you Marcus, for a moment there, I thought that was your way of *getting out.* To become a legend. Leave the game on top, you know," I confess.

"Leave? To go *where* exactly? And to do *what*?" asks Marcus, now kind of amused.

"I don't know. Gardening and stuff?" I tell him.

"Nolan, you and I both know we could never live in the normal world. It's way too slow."

Champion's got a point.

"So tell me now. That night, on the yacht. How did you do it?" I ask, fishing for more answers. "How did you manage to disappear?"

"You guys were all pretty wired up. All I had to do was to create a distraction," Marcus recounts. "So I threw some big chair overboard. Then everyone came looking for the splash."

"This I managed to piece together. But how did you get *off* the boat?" I press on.

"After I bought the scorpion painting from the auction, I put the hotel address and the room number on the delivery slip," Marcus details. "Then in the confusion of the splash, I slipped into the wooden crate, and hid there until the party was over. The next morning, they delivered me straight to my door."

"That's so simple and *cliché*," I admit with a smirk.

"And yet, that's why it worked so well."

I pace the room for a moment to take it all in. It's a beautiful day outside. Down in the hangar, the mechanics and crews from all the teams are busy packing up the trucks to get the circus back on the road again. The first wave of guests check out of the hotel suites. The second batch, still hungover, will do the same at around noon. Helicopters flying in reverse.

This small rock will be able to breathe again. And we'll all meet up next weekend on a different continent.

"Tell me, Marcus, because I need to know. How did you convince Natalia to move to your side?" I ask.

"Natalia? She was *always* on my side," Marcus says, kinda surprised.

"Wait. I thought she was working for Angelo?"

"No, see, I'm the one who hired Natalia to keep you distracted. Something shiny enough for you to chase all the way into the second act, while I was performing my disappearance," Marcus explains.

"You son of a gun!"

"By the way, she says *hello* and *sorry.*"

"Now I wish the bad guys actually kidnapped and tortured you," I joke a bit.

Marcus laughs and then stops— motioning pain in his chest.

"Are you alright, man?" I ask.

"Yeah, yeah. Let's bring everybody in. Let's get this over with, shall we?" he says.

The French doors of the bedroom slide wide open and Céline moves in, flanked by a dozen members of the press court. She gives me a wink.

At the same moment, I receive a message from Casino Jackie: "The check is ready. Come pick it up at the casino. You bastards."

No, I did not win the race this weekend.

But scoring second place was good enough to trigger that wager we took yesterday. Remember? Ten million, odds paying 10 to 1. Which means Billy, Céline and I are about to split three ways a booty of roughly a hundred million dollars.

Not bad for a weekend's work.

On the TV screen over the mantle, the news report says: *Emerald Tower developer falls to his death.*

Nobody just *falls* from a tower. It's a shame. I kinda liked Angelo.
He had a simple plan for a complicated world.

Photographers and journalists do their thing while the three of us stand together in the living room.

"Where are you guys going next?" Billy asks Céline.

"Tokyo," we both reply.

42

Final Image

We're all chasing something.
Whether it's in front of us or far behind.
It's hard to tell when we go in circles.

Around the track, around the world.
Around the wrong woman.

There are mornings where everything is so crisp and so clear, I can almost touch it. And there are nights so dark, we need to burn the candle both ways just to see it through.

And yet, with every lap we take, there's that feeling we're getting closer. And maybe, just maybe. If we go fast enough. There is a chance we can live forever.

In history, or in that moment.

That little bit of chance is what we're all chasing around. And don't worry too much if you haven't caught it yet. Just go for another lap. Another loop. This time only faster. With more passion. More *crazy*.

I caught it once or twice, and I gotta tell you. Once you get it, it's a slippery slope. You will try to hold on, but it's a slippery soap. Most of the time, you'll lose it all again. Expelled by the rotation.

This weekend, I was lucky enough for someone to catch me and point me back in the right direction. A course correction, so to speak.

Some of us might get stuck in a never-ending party, looking for an exit.

Others spend so much time crunching the numbers, they forget to believe in magic.

Some are so desperate for a win, they might try to rig the game.

Others are quick to flee in the chopper with no idea where to land.

And some will pretend just to be friends, when it's clear to everyone that they should be lovers.

Believe me, now I know.

And nothing will stop us now.

ives in Montreal, where he got to work in advertising, rea
ision. With a keen sense of observation and curiosity, he
ch collection of colorful characters and situations inspire
ls and adventures.

ED OF LIGHT is his first novel.

Credits
Cover design : Thomas B. Martin
Editor : Anna Bierhaus
Photo : Gabriel Lajournade